ADDRESS FOR MURDER

A MAIL CARRIER COZY MYSTERY
BOOK 2

TONYA KAPPES

ADDRESS FOR MURDER

"Lee, I'm coming in," I warned like it was going to make him answer me. "It's Bernadette, your mail carrier." I talked as if we were playing some sort of game. I weaved around the boxes, having to turn around a few times at various dead ends. "Buster was at the post office, and I just thought I'd bring him home."

The whimpering got a little louder as I made my way through the maze of boxes.

"This is gross," I muttered to myself and decided I'd call Luke about this when I'd found Lee safe and sound. "How does anyone live like this?" I let out a deep sigh.

Buster's whimper got a little louder which made me think I was getting closer. The closer I got, the more I started to hear a TV, which made me feel somewhat better. Lee had to be asleep in front of the television, and Buster probably wanted to eat.

At least, that was what I told myself.

"Lee?" My eyes focused on a pair of shoes, sticking straight up in the air, with... legs attached. The television played the morning news, and Buster was sitting next to the feet. "Lee?" I gulped and moved around the stack of boxes that covered my full view of what once was probably the living room of his home.

There, in plain view, was Lee, lying face up in the middle of the only open floorspace. His eyes were open, and his hand was outstretched in a strange open space with boxes built up around it as if something once there was now gone. Kind of like that Jenga game my family loved to play. One wrong move and they would all come tumbling down.

"Lee?" My voice cracked. My eyes stung with the tears

that were starting to collect. "Lee? Please tell me you're alive." I couldn't bring my focus off the stamp Lee had in his open palm. It was the stamp I'd given him yesterday from my dad.

My head dipped when I noticed no movement from Lee, and my heart sank when Buster licked his beloved owner's cold face.

Acknowledgments

Thank you to the amazing beta readers! I'm beyond thrilled I have nine amazing and talented friends who love and care for all of my cozy mysteries!

I'd also like to thank Mariah Sinclair for the vision and clarity as she brings life to all my covers.

Thank you to Red Adept Editing for the wonderful editing job you do to make my words make sense.

And a huge thank you to my husband Eddy. He does all the things that would normally take me away from writing. Without him by my side, I'd not be able to be a full time writer and fulfill my dream.

GET FREE BOOKS

Join Tonya's newsletter to stay up to date with new releases, get access to exclusive bonus content, and more!

Join Tonya's newsletter.
See all of Tonya's books.
Join all the fun on her Reader Group on Facebook.

Chapter 1

"Mornin', Bernie." Vivian Tillett greeted me as soon as I walked through the sliding double doors of the nursing home, the first stop in my mail route. "It looks like the weather is going to cooperate for you today."

"Yes." I smiled and took the mail bag off my shoulder. I set the bag on the floor between my legs. "I heard from Lucy Drake's weather report it might actually be the turn we've been waiting for."

The weather was finicky in our small town of Sugar Creek Gap. One minute it could be sunny, and the next it might be raining. Bursts of snow were not unusual. Even though I had a walking route, I really did enjoy the change in seasons, but the transition from winter to spring always did seem to be the most confusing as far as deciding what to wear for my job.

"I'll put your usual mail in your office, but you did get some magazines I know you like to keep out here for people to thumb through." I dug down into the bag and pulled out the newest editions of *Southern Living Magazine*, *Country Living*, and *Kentucky Senior Living*.

"Oh, I think we have a spotlight in here." Vivian flipped through the magazine. "Since we have gone all out for this Make Kentucky Colorful spring campaign, they featured the nursing home."

"That's so cool." I had to force myself to come up with a positive comment about this whole spring campaign that put the entire town on the crazy train. Especially the Sugar Creek Gap beautification committee. Every time I walk past someone on the committee, they ask me questions about the citizens on my route and if they've planted the flowers, cleaned up their yard, or taken down ugly yard ornaments.

"I-32!" my friend, Iris Peabody, shouted from the main dining room of the nursing home, which was adjacent to where I stood with Vivian. "I-32!"

"Bingo?" I asked Vivian, hoisting the bag off the ground and up on my shoulder.

"Yes. Everyone is in there today." Vivian's attention turned from the magazine to the opening sliding glass doors.

"Hey, Luke," I said with a nod when Luke Macum walked up to me and Vivian.

He was a big man, full-chested and brown-haired. He looked very distinguished with sparkling blue eyes. Today might be the first time I'd ever seen Luke Macum dressed down in a pullover sweater with three large wooden buttons. Though they weren't buttoned, he still looked very dapper.

"Hey there, Bernie." He gave a hint of a smile. "Have you been by my uncle's yet?"

"No. This is my first stop." The nursing home was right behind the post office, making it easier for me to stop here since I had so much mail to deliver to both the residences and the low-maintenance housing for senior citizens without any health problems, who lived in the condominiums on the property. "I'll head over his way in a couple of hours."

"I'm getting ready to head on over there if you just want to give me his mail." Luke made a nice gesture, and his idea would have been good if it weren't slightly illegal.

"That's nice of you, but I don't even have Little Creek Road's mail in here." I patted the bag dangling off my shoulder.

I had a three-mail loop every day. The first loop in my bag was the nursing home. The second loop consisted of all the shops located on Main Street and Little Creek Road residence because there were only a few houses on the dead end street. Then I finished my day with the neighborhood located behind the Old Mill downtown.

Since my route was downtown and the houses were located around here, it was easier for me to walk back to the post office between loops than to drive an LLV, a lifelong vehicle.

"Thanks anyways." I tapped the counter and turned back to Vivian. "I'm going to head in and see everyone before I go fill up the mailboxes."

"B-12! B-12!" Iris's voice carried into the hallway. She was looking around the large dining room when I leaned up against the door taking in all the folks who were busy with their eyes on their bingo cards. I'd never seen such a large group of women be so quiet, but when a bingo was up for grabs, it was a big deal around here. "B-12!"

When our eyes caught, I waved, half expecting a wave back, but instead she gave a huge hand gesture for me to come up there.

"Come here," she mouthed. Then she realized the microphone was still in her hand. "Come here, Bernie," she said into the device.

I pushed off the door jamb and couldn't help but overhear Luke talking to Vivian.

"I don't know what the signs are, but he's starting to misplace things. He's not keeping himself clean. I don't even think he's eating." Luke sounded very concerned. "I'm the only kin he's got, and I'm worried."

He was obviously talking about his uncle, Mr. Macum, who he'd offered to take the mail.

I'd made a mental note to grab something homemade from my parents' diner when I delivered their mail and offer it to Mr. Macum when I dropped off the mail for him. The weather wasn't what made my job as a mail carrier hard. Seeing my customers grow older each year was what tugged at my heart.

Instead of standing there eavesdropping, I weaved in and out of the big round tables on my way up to the front to talk to Iris.

"What did she call?" a woman at one of the tables asked her friend.

"B-12!" her friend yelled into her ear.

"D-12?" she asked and ran her finger along her card.

"No. B! B as in boy!" The friend grabbed the card and held it up close to her eyes.

Apparently, one could hear and the other could see. Each helped the other with the skills she had lost in her elderly years. They were exactly how I pictured Iris and me.

"Bernadette, is that you?" I heard a small voice call to me when I passed by.

I looked over, careful not to hit anyone with the mail bag, and noticed one of my customers from the last neighborhood I delivered to.

"Mrs. Clark." I was shocked to see her here. "What are you doing here?"

"Oh, honey. Them young 'uns of mine. They figured I needed some help after I took a few tumbles over the winter." She shook her head, making the blue tint of her hair glow from underneath the lights in the dining room. "Instead of them fussing over who was going to take care of me and whose house I was going to live in, I just called Walter Ward and had him put my house up for sale and decided to move myself in here."

"I'm so glad to know you've done what you think is best for yourself." I could count over a dozen elderly people in this very room whose families had them placed in the nursing home. "I'm sure your house is going to sell very fast."

It took every part of my being not to ask why she put her beloved home in the hands of Walter Ward. He was a good real estate agent but didn't have a moral bone in his body.

"I hope so." She looked up and over the edges of her glasses. "This place ain't cheap."

"I'll be sure to make an extra special stop when I'm delivering mail to come visit." That was why I made the nursing home my first stop.

The residents of the nursing home were always up before the rooster crowed, waiting for their mail, and always eager for company. Plus, the place was always open, unlike the shops, which all opened at nine a.m.

"You do that, honey." Mrs. Clark went back to her bingo card.

There were a few hellos and how-are-yous as I continued to make my way up to Iris, who was still calling out the bingo letters.

"Tell me why I volunteer for this?" she asked me, putting the microphone down on the table next to the cage with the bingo ping-pong balls in it.

"Because we might have to be in here one day and we want to be taken care of like you take care of them." I held true to the idea that if you gave out goodness, it came back to you tenfold.

"Speaking of being taken care of…" Her eyes grew bigger. She had that look.

"Oh no." I put my hand up and shook my head. "I don't want to know."

You see, Iris claims to get these feelings. Feelings about people. She's not psychic or anything, but she'd ask about someone we hadn't heard from or even thought of in a long time, and then either we'd run into that person or hear something about them. It was something very strange, but it was Iris.

She'd been doing it since we were in grade school. Only a handful of times had she gotten it right. The first was when my husband Richard had been killed in a car wreck. Over ten years ago she got a feeling that something was wrong with him. Dead wrong.

Then there was an unfortunate event last year when she had a bad feeling about Mac Tabor, which turned out to be somewhat true. Still…I didn't have time to hear this today.

"There's something about Little Creek Road." She shifted, sticking her hands on her hips. Her long, curly brown hair had elegant gray streaks and was pulled up in a top knot on the crown of her head. "My last feeling…"

"Don't remind me." Again, Mac lived on Little Creek Road. "I'll keep an eye out on my way over there." I gave her a quick hug, knowing this feeling was why she'd called me up here in the first place. "I've got to get hustling or I'll never get the mail delivered."

"Fine. Don't forget you said you'd help me finish off the cookies for Carla Ramey." She reminded me how

Carla had hired Pie in the Face, Iris's bake shop, to make the cookies for the big reception for the Make Kentucky Colorful spring campaign. Carla had also hired the shop to make the cake for her retirement, which was going to be celebrated at the same reception. Carla was the president of the beautification committee and had been for as long as I could remember.

"I didn't forget," I called over my shoulder on my way back out of the dining room.

"Take a look around," Iris blurted out. She gestured a circle around the room with her finger. "This is going to be you and me in twenty years."

I laughed. Iris was always reminding me we were now in our fifties.

Luke and Vivian had moved from the entrance to her office, which was just on the right side. Her office was glass, and the blinds were pulled open, allowing me to see the inside, where she was showing him some brochures.

Then… I couldn't help but wonder if Iris was talking about Mr. Macum. Was it a coincidence Luke was here and that Mr. Macum lived on Little Creek Road?

I shoved out any bad thoughts out of my head and headed to the community mailboxes to finish up my time there at the nursing home.

Chapter 2

"What on earth is she doing?" I asked Monica Reed as we stood in the parking lot of the post office. I'd just filled my mail bag with the second loop, which consisted of the downtown shops and government offices along with the dead-end neighborhood of Little Creek Road.

Monica craned her neck around me to look at Carla, who had jumped out of her car with her hand gripped around the handle of some sort of bottle. With her other hand, she sprayed something out of that bottle into the cracks of the sidewalk.

"Is she spraying the weeds in the cracks?" I narrowed my eyes to get a good look, pushing back a strand of my auburn hair that'd fallen out of my low ponytail. "Oh my God, I think she is."

"This whole beautification thing has made her lose the good sense God gave her." Monica *tsk*ed and went back to checking out the LLVs for the carriers who did drive.

Monica was the post-office clerk. She was always the first one there, sorting mail and certified letters that needed to be delivered. She also helped the drivers each morning check out their LLV before they headed out on their routes.

"I swear." I shook my head and headed off in the direction of Main Street. "I'll see you in a few hours." I waved goodbye to Monica but couldn't help but laugh when I saw Carla jump out of her car again to squirt more weeds.

The street was starting to come alive with cars and a few citizens walking down the street. I quickly delivered the mail to the Doctor Building, which was next to the post office, and then the Sugar Creek Gap Bank next to that. Next, I crossed the street to deliver the mail back to back to the locally owned shops.

"Good morning, Bernie." Leotta Goldey greeted me when I walked into Social Knitwork. "It's going to be a gorgeous day," she called from over her shoulder from the display window of her yarn shop. She pointed. "Can you hand me the tape? It's on the counter."

I dropped my mail bag next to the counter and picked up the tape. Then I took it to her.

"Carla dropped off this participation certificate and wants all of us to tape it on our display windows for the judges to see." She drew a long breath. "I'll be so glad when this is over."

"I swear I just saw her jump out of her car and put weed killer on the sidewalk cracks." I went back to my mail bag, dug out Leotta's mail, and then placed it in the basket next to the register.

"No weed will live from Carla's determined-to-win eye," Leotta joked, only it was true.

"No outgoing?" It was common for the shop owners not to have gotten their mail ready before I'd arrived, since I was there when they first opened.

"Not a thing." She backed out of the display window.

"Your window is amazing." My eyes feasted on the old bike.

The bike had a wire basket on the front filled with various bright colors of yarn balls. Tin flower holders filled with yarn flowers in the colors of spring hung off the bike's back wire shelf. She had made at least eight butterflies of different sizes out of yarn and hung them with fishing wire from the ceiling. The sight was amazing.

"Thank you. I spent a lot of time on it because I didn't want to have Carla on my back like she's been doing to all the neighbors." Leotta rolled her eyes. "How is Julia's blanket coming along?"

"I forgot all about that. I don't know." Over the past couple of months, Leotta had kept asking me about a blanket Julia, my daughter-in-law, had been making in one of Leotta's knitting classes. "I'll be sure to ask when I see her this morning."

As the mail carrier of most of the businesses in Sugar Creek Gap, I tended to see everyone every day, including my parents, who owned Wallflower Diner, and Julia, the secretary for Tabor Construction.

The bell over the shop door dinged. A few women with a bag filled to the top with yarn and knitting needles sticking out headed straight to the next room, where Leotta taught classes, and sat their bags down on the table.

"Good morning, ladies. Are you ready for class?" Leotta turned her attention to them while I headed out the door and got back on the sidewalk, where I quickly delivered mail to Tranquility Wellness, the locally owned spa and yoga studio.

I always gave myself a good minute while I was in there to take a few deep breaths, since the place smelled so good, even though I knew the perfect spa smell that made me feel all zen was chemically made and piped into the ventilation system.

But it was the smell of my mom's freshly made biscuits that really made me feel at home when I walked into the Wallflower Diner.

It was a typical diner with metal tables and red vinyl metal chairs that took up the interior flooring. They had saltshakers filled with salt and a few pieces of elbow macaroni—which kept the salt fresh, according to my mom—along with matching pepper shakers. They also had fresh cream on the tables for the coffee drinkers. A small bud vase with a plastic red rose and the menu pushed between the bud vase and shakers.

"There's my baby girl." My dad waved me over to the counter, where he was having his morning meeting with the local men who gathered there every day.

"Y'all solving all the world's problems?" I asked and pulled my mail bag around to my front so I could get the diner mail out. I handed it to my dad.

"Just trying to figure out what we are going to do with Carla." Dad nodded swiftly over to the few tables that'd been pushed together. "She's over there telling them they need to go door to door in all the neighborhoods to make sure everyone has a flyer in their window and their yards all dolled up with flowers."

Carla was over there with what looked like the members of the beautification committee.

"Hi, dear." Mom walked out of the kitchen passthrough, rubbing her hands off on the apron tied around her waist. "How are you this morning?"

"I'm good, Mom." We hugged and kissed cheeks. "How about you?"

"You know, kneading the dough." She winked and grabbed a ceramic mug from behind the counter. In one fluid motion, she'd set the mug down in front of me and already started to pour me a cup of coffee. "Go on. Sit down. Warm up your bones. It might look nice outside, but there's still a chill in the air, and I can't have you catching cold."

I was never one to protest against my mom. She always won.

"And I'll get you a fresh biscuit." She didn't even bother letting me decline the biscuit. She headed straight back into the kitchen and soon came back with a golden-brown biscuit topped with a pat of butter that was melting faster than she could set it down in front of me. "Tell me what you've been up to," she said and leaned on the counter, like we didn't see each other a few times a day.

"Same thing as last time I saw you." I picked up the biscuit and took a bite. "Can I get a few biscuits to go? I want them for Mr. Macum."

"Put some arsenic in those biscuits. Then he won't be the bane of my existence." Carla came out of nowhere and nudged me with a giggle.

"Carla Ramey, that's not so nice," I told her and looked into her black eyes to determine whether she was kidding or serious—or what even possessed her to say something so mean. "He's a nice man."

"Nice man? He and I are at odds, and if we lose the Make Kentucky Colorful campaign, it'll all be because of him." She put her money and food bill on the counter next me. "Mark my words."

"You know that old washtub leaning up on the side of his house?" One of my dad's friends leaned on his forearms to look down the counter from the stool he was sitting on. He continued, "That was my old washtub from five years ago."

"Mmm-hhhmm." Carla's lips pinched. "He picked up

any old thing when he was picking up trash, but now that he's retired, he needs to clean up that yard. I can't tell you how many times the city has cited him."

"From what I heard, he picks up just enough not to be in violation." The man shrugged and picked up his coffee cup to take a drink. "No problem to me. He ain't hurting no one."

"His hoarding is hurting my legacy. I've spent my entire life for this community, and here is my last hurrah to get some sort of award before I retire. I'll be dang sure it won't be Lee Macum who keeps me from it."

Carla turned on the toes of her shoes and stalked straight out of the diner, leaving me, Mom, Dad, and a few others shaking our heads until the door shut.

Chapter 3

There would not be enough cups of coffee or time spent at the diner to stall the next stop on my route—Tabor Architects, owned by Mac Tabor.

Mac was Richard's best friend and had taken great interest in making sure my family had been well taken care of since Richard's death. Mac had also gone to great lengths to ensure Richard's long-time affair and possible love child had been kept a secret even after the ten years of Richard's death. Lucky for Grady and me, the child Richard's lover had wasn't his, and it was a chapter in my life I'd completely let go of, but Mac hadn't.

Mac was still a big part of the community and my life. It didn't help that we had an obvious attraction to one another. Over the past couple of months, we'd been tiptoeing around it when we were together. Though the feelings were there, and other people had even commented on them, we'd yet to make good on them and pretended all the little things he did for me were just part of his promise to Richard to keep Grady and me safe and happy.

Richard even hired Julia as his secretary, not only

paying her a hefty salary but giving her a nice insurance policy, stock options, and all the things he would to his own daughter-in-law.

"I have a treat for you." I took out one of the to-go bags my mom had given me for the various residents she loved to send biscuits to and put it on Julia's desk. "Grandma sent a treat over to hold you until lunch. She said you rushed out of there."

Julia and Grady lived in the apartment over the diner, which was a nice arrangement, since they both worked close by.

Grady was the English teacher and the head football coach at the Sugar Creek Gap High School. And now that football season was over, I got to see my baby more, and I loved that.

"I had to get to work because Mac told Carla he'd help in any way he could." Julia took the biscuit out of the bag and went to town on it. I'd never seen her eat so fast. "These are so good," she said through a muffled mouthful of biscuit.

"Mac's not here?" I asked, feeling a little more relaxed.

"No." A big smile curled up on her face. "You just missed him. Carla ran in here and got him saying something about Lee Macum, Walter Ward, and the houses."

I knew exactly what she was talking about. Mac lived a few houses away from Lee Macum and recently purchased the two homes next to Lee's home—one he was using Walter as a real estate agent to sell and the other he was working on as a rehab.

"I wouldn't put it past her to have Mac do something about his houses." I took the mail for Tabor Architects out of my bag and handed it to Julia. "How are you?"

"Me?" She jerked up and looked at me. "I'm fine. Why

do you ask?" She seemed a little flustered or taken aback that I'd even ask such a thing.

"I'm just checking on you. Grady's been over a few times to the house without you, and he just said you've been tired from working." I tossed my bag over my shoulder and noticed the bag of yarn and needles on the floor next to Julia's desk.

"I'm good. I'm fine." She blew me off, knocking the bag under the desk with her shoe like I didn't see it. She leaned around me to look at the door.

"Hey, you." Mac Tabor stood right behind me. His thick brown hair was perfectly styled. His big brown eyes danced as they moved around my face, and that smile... It sent my toes curling. "I was going to call you today. But here you are."

"Here I am." I rocked back on the thick soles of my mail carrier shoes and felt like a complete idiot. I was a fifty-year-old woman feeling like a twenty-something looking at a crush.

Since discovering Richard's horrible affair, I'd long forgiven myself for these underlying feelings for Mac and actually given myself permission to feel them as long as the town didn't know about them. I heard so much gossip on my route. I could only imagine what the gossip would be like if it was about me.

"I've been wanting to try that new Italian place for supper. I wanted to know if you'd like to go with me tonight?" As he spoke, I could feel Julia's stare behind me.

"Tonight?" I asked as if I had something to do, which I did not.

"Dinner tonight?" His smile reached the corners of his eyes.

The door flew open, and Walter Ward walked in, saving me from the bumbling fool I felt like I was being—

although Walter Ward wasn't my favorite person in Sugar Creek Gap. In fact, Richard was no longer among the living, and Walter Ward quickly put his foot in my living room. Did I think he was giving me some sincere condolences? No, he was looking around assessing my home for a good market value because, according to him, I wouldn't be able to keep up with the place.

"We've got a problem." Walter tapped Mac on the front of his shoulder. "Rats. I was showing your house to a potential client, and lo and behold"—Walter drew his arms open in front of him—"rats in the basement. Those buyers hightailed it out of there and couldn't drive their car fast enough off Little Creek Road. I've never been so embarrassed in my life." He smoothed a smudge of his mustache with a ring-laden finger.

Even if he'd not set foot into my home hours after Richard had died, I still wouldn't have trusted him. Lord knew I wasn't one to judge, but I'd seen too many of my elderly neighbors either pass away or relocate to the nursing home, only for Walter Ward to show up seconds later… like an ambulance chaser.

"Rats?" Mac suddenly went into business mode as I'd seen him do so many times. "Where are they coming from?"

"You really need to ask that?" Walter suddenly noticed me. "Bernadette," he greeted me. "Did I interrupt something?" He looked between Mac and me.

"No." I shook my head.

"You sure did," Mac said over me. "I was just asking Bernie to supper at the new Italian place."

"Oh yeah. Me and the missus went. So good." Walter licked his lips as if he remembered. "The rats?" He looked at Mac.

"Just take care of it," Mac told him.

"I'll go take care of it, and tomorrow you have those flowers there and ready." He pointed at Mac. "Not only will they make the house look pretty, it'll keep Carla Ramey off my back. She's been over there fussing about Lee's house and beating his door down. His poor dog has been barking all day at her, but she keeps showing up."

"What is Lee saying to her?" Mac asked. When I took a few steps to head back to my mail route, he stuck his hand out and gently touched my forearm for me to wait a second. He looked at me and smiled.

"He won't open the door. He keeps pulling the blind back and eyeballing her with one eye." Walter's visual made me laugh only because I'd been on the receiving end of that eye when I delivered his mail or when he got a certified letter. "I'll go fix the problem." Walter made his statement sound like code talk before he headed out of the office.

"How about if I pick you up and we go pick out a few flowers then go eat." He could see my hesitation and started to talk some more. "I need a woman's touch. What do you say?"

"Yeah. Sure." I smiled and couldn't help but see Julia's great big grin from the corner of my eye.

I couldn't get out of there any faster.

As I took in some deep breaths and saw the signs of spring on the horizon, it didn't take long for my heart rate to go back to normal and for me to get into the delivery mail groove. The winter months were long in Kentucky, and they really didn't clear up for another month or so, but the trees were showing signs of buds on their otherwise bare branches, and some green stems sprang up through the mulch in my clients' yards.

But the biggest sign that spring was coming was from my duck friend who lived on the bridge that connected my route from Short Street to Little Creek Road. He was there all year long but was more active in the creek that ran between the backs of the downtown shops and the Little Creek Road neighborhood.

Quack, quack. He greeted me with his usual duck tone and swam around in a couple of circles until I stopped at the middle of the bridge. I swear he knew it was me from the sound of my big-soled mail carrier shoes. We weren't required to wear these shoes, but they were made for a reason. They had good padding, and trust me when I tell people just how much mail carriers' feet and toes take a beating. It's ugly, and a good pedicure does nothing for them.

I reached around and grabbed one of the few biscuit boxes my mom had given me, and I quickly pinched a piece off for the duck. It was probably something Carla Ramey would just drop dead and die if she saw because she'd say it was bad not only for the duck but also for the creek.

"You gotta live a little," I told my duck friend when I tossed the piece of biscuit over the bridge and right in front of him. "A little bit of bad food isn't going hurt." I reached around for the rest of the biscuit. "See." I stuffed the rest in my mouth.

He gobbled it up and did his usual laps until he headed down the creek, which was where he'd meet me again for another little pinch of whatever I had in my bag. Little Creek Road was a dead-end street with nine houses along the right side. Looking down the street, I saw they all stood like soldiers with their uniform fences, gates, small front yards with sidewalks up the middle, and three steps up to covered brick porches with half-brick walls.

At each end of the street was a bridge. The bridge at the very end of the dead end connected to Main Street but was only a walking bridge. After I delivered the mail to the nine houses, I met my duck friend for one last hurrah for the day and then headed over the bridge to the post office, where I picked up my last loop and started on the longest part of my route.

The first house on Little Creek Road belonged to Mac Tabor. Just thinking about him and our... well... date was probably not what he had in mind, but technically it was dinner, so we would just call it that. Anyway, thinking about it made me jittery, so I took another deep breath and blew out a long stream of air out of my mouth.

I put my hand on the latch of his gate and clicked it open. Mac generally didn't get a whole lot of personal mail, but he did get various architecture magazines. All the mailboxes were built into the brick wall near the front door of each house.

Sugar Creek Gap was built around the Old Mill, which was founded in the old mining days. Some of these houses were built way back then and were protected by the Sugar Creek Gap Historical Society, of which I was a member, and it was an act of Congress to get anything approved if you wanted any sort of renovations on your house. The historical society was one thing Mac would complain about as an architect, but on the flip side, she loved how they built back in the day.

When the two houses next to Mr. Macum came up for sale, Mac had bought them. He did all the due diligence and filed the various permits to get the historical society to rehabilitate the inside without hurting the structure.

The one next to Mr. Macum was all ready to sell, and Walter Ward was the realtor for that one. The other was two doors away from Mr. Macum, and he'd not yet finished it. Some of his permits had yet to come back, so I was sure that was why.

I dropped my mail bag and dug out his mail, pushing it through the slot.

"Mornin', Bernie!"

I glanced up and saw Harriette Pearl waving from next door. She had her fluffy mint green house coat tightly snuggled around her thick waist. Her hair was still in curlers, and she held a cup of coffee in her hand.

"Anything good for me today?" she asked.

"I don't know." I tugged my bag up on my shoulder and made my way out of Mac's yard, happy for the distraction of Harriette's conversation and temporarily forgetting about my dinner with Mac.

"I'm hoping to get an invitation to Zeke Grey's bridal shower he's hosting for his soon-to-be-granddaughter-in-law. I heard they went out a couple of days ago," she said and moved to the top step of her porch to wait for me.

"Oh. That's delightful. I'd not seen any signs of an invitation today." I walked up the sidewalk and the steps. I put the mail bag down to retrieve her stack of mail. "It's unusual for a granddaughter to have a bridal shower, much less for a man to host it."

"Let me grab you a coffee." Harriette didn't bother letting me protest. Getting me something to drink was her usual activity depending on the time of day and the time of year. She seemed to enjoy keeping me hydrated. "I'll tell you all about it. Not that I'm gossiping or anything."

If it were a little hotter, she'd have a thermos full of ice-cold sweet tea, but today there was still a bit of chill in the morning air from the change in seasons.

"Hello, Bernadette." Ruby Dean walked up Harriette's sidewalk followed closely by Gertrude Stone and Millie Barnes.

"The gang's all here." I smiled as each one of them

filed up the steps and took their usual perch on Harriette's porch.

Ruby liked to sit in the rocking chair opposite Harriette's rocking chair. The backs of both chairs faced Mac's home. The wooden swing opposite the porch and facing Mac's house was where Gertrude and Millie liked to sit, while I took a hinny lean on the half-brick wall of the porch.

"Anything new?" Ruby asked as if I should know something.

"Should there be?" I gave her the side-eye.

"I was wondering when y'all were coming over here." Harriette brought out an entire pot of coffee sitting on a tray with teetering coffee cups. "Did you ask?"

"Ask me what?" I knew Harriette was asking about me.

"About the invitations." Harriette reminded me of the bridal shower invitation.

"We just got here, Harriette," Gertrude said between her gritted teeth. Then she turned to me, planting a big smile on her face. "Bernie needs a rest. She's been walking all morning."

"Did you use the foot massage lotion I gave you for Christmas?" Millie asked.

"I haven't gotten a chance to do that yet, but I plan on taking a couple days off after spring really arrives." My brows rose. "That's when I'm going to be doing a full day for me. Including the foot cream you gave me and the masks Ruby gave me, along with the hand scrub Gertrude gave me."

"After you're all prettied up, you can take Mac to supper on the gift card that I gave you." Harriette wasn't one to be left out.

"Mac?" I asked. I'd not mentioned Mac to anyone but Iris. Maybe my family had seen how Mac had acted right before Christmas, but we'd not been around them altogether for a while.

Sure, he would do what I called conveniently stopping by the farmhouse on Sunday family supper night, but I never recalled him actually acting as if he were interested in me. Besides, my parents were older, and they never caught on to things like that. Plus, Grady and Julia still acted as if the world revolved around them, so I knew they didn't see anything… if there was anything. For all I knew, this little supper Mac had asked me out to tonight was no different from the friends thing we'd been doing for the past ten years.

"Bernadette." Harriette waved her hand in front of me. "I don't know where you just drifted off to, but your coffee is going to get cold."

"Don't rush her." Ruby's gaze darted to Harriette. "She's got plenty of time to sit here. Bernie, you can just hand us our mail. That way, you don't have to walk all the way down there."

"Are you sure?" I asked even though it would be nice to just hand them their mail while they were here. "I still have to go to Mr. Macum's."

"Lee." Gertrude groaned when she called Mr. Macum by his name, then she followed up with a *tsk*. "That man. He got another notice from the city to clean up his property, and he doesn't care one iota."

"Carla Ramey cares an iota. A big iota."

"I nearly forgot." Their mention of Carla Ramey made me think of the biscuits my mom had sent with me to give to the gals. I reached down into my bag and pulled out the box, handing it to Gertrude. "Mom says to tell you ladies hello."

"Your mama. She's a good one." Ruby did the gimmie

hand when I passed the box to Gertrude. "You're just like her."

"Now what about the invitation?" Harriette brought the discussion back to the mail.

"Who got invited and who didn't?" Gertrude was on the edge of the swing with her feet firmly planted on the porch. Her eyes snapped. She crossed her arms, impatiently waiting for me to answer.

"To tell you the truth, I don't really look that closely at anyone's mail, but I do generally take notice if several people on my route are getting the same envelope." Not all of that was entirely true. I did have a slightly nosy side, but it was completely against the code of ethics according to the United States Postal Service.

In this case, I'd yet to see any sort of invitation, so that wasn't a lie.

"Here is Harriette's mail." I pulled out her new *Reader's Digest*, *Hollywood Reporter*, and the local coupon magazine along with a few more pieces of junk mail.

While she thumbed through that, I took all the other front porch ladies' mail out one by one and distributed it to them. Each of them hurried to look for this prize invitation to the bridal shower.

"I really can't believe Zeke is hosting this." He was about the front porch ladies' age and a town council member who was a long-time widower. He was in a lot of clubs, including the bridge club all these ladies were in. I only knew this because I delivered his mail.

His neighborhood was on my third loop, and it was about the right time for him to be home and want to talk. Though he didn't feel like he was a gossip, he was the biggest one. He was just like these women.

"You know how close he is with Robby," Ruby said,

mentioning the grandson. "The bride isn't from here, so Zeke is hosting a party at the country club."

"So it'll be all swanky." Millie's shoulders lifted toward her ears, and a delighted look came to her face.

"When I get mine, I'm going right on down to Barb's Beauty and getting me a fresh perm," said Ruby. "I don't care, even if it is before my annual spring appointment."

"What makes you so sure you're going to get an invitation over me?" Gertrude had taken offense. "I'm the one who helped Zeke with all the new decks of cards for the bridge club by using my Amazon Prime account."

"What about me?" Millie inhaled a sharp breath. "When Zeke was sick, I let everyone come to my house for bridge club. Not to mention I made him some of my delicious corn chowder." She crossed her tiny arms across her body. "It was my own mother's secret recipe too. Not some store-bought stuff in a can."

The ladies continued to argue. They were like the kids from the Willy Wonka movie, squabbling over who was going to get the golden ticket. I had a niggling suspicion they were all vying for more than an invitation to a bridal shower.

"Yoo-hoo!" a voice called out from the passing car along with a little beep.

All of us looked up and saw Carla Ramey beeping and waving like a wild woman, not bothering to slow down.

"Oh geez." Harriette's nose curled. "It's gonna be a bad day on Little Creek Road now."

"Yeah, I was hoping she'd stay on her side of downtown." Gertrude's head turned as she watched Carla's car drive past.

I didn't have to ask to know what they meant by her side of downtown. Carla lived in the neighborhood right behind the courthouse on the other side of Main Street.

Her house was included in my third and final loop, which ended my day.

"Are you kidding? She's all gone crazy over this Kentucky Colorful...or whatever it is." Ruby waved her hand around and rolled her eyes. "She's been coming over here every day to beat on Lee's door about cleaning up his yard."

"She's been personally taking the tickets the city is issuing him to his house. When he doesn't answer, she bangs more and yells through the door about the fine." Harriette *tsk*ed. "You know"—Ruby leaned forward a little in the rocking chair and nodded her chin slightly in Millie's direction—"some of us are hard of hearing and she even heard it."

"What did you say?" Millie's brows furrowed, and I could see her eyes were focused on Ruby's lips.

"They were just saying how Lee is a hoarder." I didn't want to cause any rift between the friends. They already bickered back and forth so much. I pushed myself up to stand and took one more drink before I hoisted my bag back up on my shoulder. "I've got to get going."

"Bernie, now you keep an eye out for those invitations." Harriette acted as if I were her personal gossip line.

"I'll keep an eye out." I winked. "You ladies have a nice day. It just might warm up to the fifties."

They all mumbled their goodbyes and then started discussing the bridal shower. Once I was back on the sidewalk and heading toward Mr. Macum's home, Carla's banging was echoing throughout the neighborhood.

I turned to look over my shoulder at the front porch ladies. All of them were standing up, looking down the street at the noise.

"We told you she's lost her mind!" Gertrude Stone lifted her mug in the air and yelled my way.

Without saying a word, I continued down the sidewalk, but by the time I made it past all the front porch ladies' houses, Carla had jumped in her car and made a U-turn at the end of the street, nearly missing hitting the car coming down the street.

The big Buick was Walter Ward's, and he pulled up to the curb in front of the house he was selling for Mac, which was right next to Mr. Macum's house.

Carla saw me, swerved the car across the street, and threw the vehicle in park. I quickly stopped when I noticed she was gesturing for me to hold on.

"You better watch where you're going!" Walter shouted to Carla when she got out of her car and ran over to me on the sidewalk. "You're gonna kill someone!"

"You're dang straight!" she yelled back, pumping her fist in the air. "I'm gonna kill Lee Macum!"

Walter shook his head and went on in the front gate of the house, carrying two plastic jugs of something I couldn't make out from where I was standing.

"I'm so glad I caught you." Carla had a bag in her grip. "I know you'll be working the day the judges are visiting Sugar Creek Gap for the big contest. They might see you, and they might not." She stuck the bag out for me to take. "I've gone to the liberty to get you some battery-operated twinkle lights along with some extra batteries and a couple of pots and hangers with a few plants in my trunk."

"Huh?" I looked at her.

"What do you mean 'huh'?" she said mockingly and snapped her beady eyes at me. "You're going to get the pull mail cart that day and decorate your cart. It's all for the greater good of our town, Bernadette Butler." She scolded me, "You of all citizens should know that. You see every house on your route and how gorgeous… well." She hesitated and slid her glare at Mr. Macum's house. "Ninety-nine point nine percent of all houses have taken pride in Sugar Creek Gap, and you are no exception. I know you live in the country and this is the city, but you are as much of a fixture in town as the Wallflower Diner."

Carla was really selling the importance of my job to me. Boy, did I know. I didn't need her to tell me. I needed her to move so I could get on with delivering the mail. Then I decided to just agree, take the bag, and get on with my day.

"No problem." I took the bag and forced a grin. "I'll be more than happy to do my little part for Sugar Creek Gap."

"Now"—she stuck her hand on her hips—"why can't everyone be so agreeable?" She let out a long sigh. She didn't have to name who she was talking about. Apparently, everyone in town already knew. "The day of the judging, I'll just drop these off with Matilda, and she can have them waiting for you when you get to the post office."

"I'm sure she's going to love seeing you so early." I took a couple of steps forward before she stopped me again.

"And if you get to see Lee today when you deliver his mail, tell him that I'm not going to let him ruin my chances of winning…. Ahem." She cleared her throat. "Our chances of winning."

"Will do." I certainly would not. She didn't need to know that.

My response must've been good enough for her because she hurried back to her car but not without getting one last look at Lee Macum's house, which, I had to admit, had gotten much worse over the winter months.

It was as if he'd taken in the things that he really loved and when the snow started to melt, he put them back out on the porch.

28

I couldn't help but feel somewhat bad for him. The only family he had around here was Lucas, and he'd retired from the garbage company.

I remember when he did work. He got off about the time I was finishing up the other neighborhood and walking back towards town. His old beat-up truck was piled high with junk that he'd collected that day on his garbage route. He called those objects his treasures. It didn't bother me any, I was glad just to know those things made him happy.

I wasn't so concerned about his house or even his junked-up yard as much as what I'd seen and heard at the nursing home this morning. Lucas had to be talking about Mr. Macum and how he'd been getting forgetful. That just broke my heart.

"Hello again, Bernie," Walter called from the outside of the house next to Mr. Macum. "I can't believe there are rats here." He pumped one of the jugs' levers and then picked up a sprayer that was attached to the jug. "I've got to spray for rats. I bet they're coming from over there. I swear." Walter shook his head, a look of disgust crossing his face. "If Carla doesn't kill him before I do…."

I gave a half smile. Out of the corner of my eye, I saw Mr. Macum pull the curtain back from one of the side windows and peek out at us.

"He's messing with my income. I'm the realtor, and I need to sell this house." He pointed the sprayer directly at me. "You, young lady, as Mac's best friend, should tell Mr. Macum that. Maybe he will listen to you."

"I'll leave all that up to you and Mac." I waved my hand in front of my face when a whiff of the rat killer wafted my way. I wanted to warn him that if he pointed that thing at me one more time, he was going to draw back a nub, but I didn't. I kept my mouth shut because I needed my job. If I didn't have my job, I couldn't pay my bills, and then I'd have to let Walter sell my house. He'd get the last laugh…what a shame.

Buster was already barking from inside Mr. Macum's house when I got to the gate. I wasn't sure, but I thought Mr. Macum had tightened the bolts on his gate because it always took me two hands to lift the darn latch with a little force behind it. Once I finally got it open, the sound of the latch on the gate to let me in really set Buster on a barking rampage.

I was busy trying to get out the stamp I'd gotten from my dad and the biscuits Mom had sent that I didn't even hear Mr. Macum open the door.

Buster darted, bouncing toward me with his tail wagging.

"Hey, Buster." The big burly chocolate Labrador Retriever always put a smile on my face. "You know I didn't forget you." I winced from the force of his tail beating up against my thigh.

I put my hand in my coat pocket, took out one of the many dog biscuits I kept inside, and gently handed it to him. I came into contact with many furry animals during the day, and they loved me, since I had this little trick of treats.

"Good morning, Mr. Macum." I walked up the sidewalk.

"Lee, Bernie. How many times do I have to tell you, of all people, to call me Lee?" His voice cracked. I could see the darkened circles under his eyes that were a bit sunken, and his jowls were a little saggier than usual. He was definitely getting older, but he clearly remembered me.

"You tell my mom that." My mom always taught me to be respectful of my elders, and even though I was fifty, Lee was still an elder. "Speaking of my mom, she sent some homemade biscuits."

I handed him the Styrofoam container. Buster couldn't stop himself from trying to get his own smell of them.

"And my dad told me to give you this." I handed him the stamp.

He lit up like the sun when he looked at it. Lee collected stamps. Most of them had no value, but like Dad, if I noticed a really pretty stamp on a package, I'd ask the recipient—if they were home—if I could have the stamp for Mr. Macum. That led to me collecting many stamps along the way because some of my clients already had filled little baggies with Mr. Macum's name written in Sharpie on them and left them in their mailboxes or on their porches.

"You come from good stock, Bernie." Mr. Macum looked at me, and I thought he was holding back a smile. "You know, these people are driving me nuts. Driving me nuts!" he emphasized and yelled towards Walter Ward. "They need to leave me alone and mind their own business!"

I couldn't help but keep my eyes on him and not look over at Walter. You know how you can feel someone staring at you? Well, that was how it was with Walter in that exact moment. I could not only feel him looking at Mr. Macum and me, but I could hear the sound of the sprayer squirting at record speed.

Looking into Mr. Macum's dark eyes, I tried to determine whether he might be open to me mentioning a little something about cleaning up his yard. His cut his eyes at me, and I made the decision not to bring it up. It was as though he knew I was thinking of it.

"Awe, geez." Lee groaned when a truck load of Logsdon Landscapers got out and started to grab all the tools out of the truck bed, including the flowers. "Anyway, tell your parents thank you for thinking of me. It's not often people do kind things for others."

"I'll tell them." I handed him the rest of his mail and turned to leave.

"Say," he called. When I turned back around, he was thumbing through his mail. "Did you give me all my mail?"

"I did." I was pretty confident.

"I didn't get something I was expecting. You know that email digest thing I get from you where you take a photo of my mail and send it?" He referred to the daily digest the USPS had as an option for subscribers.

"I'm sorry, Lee." I needed to correct him. "I don't take the photos. That's the much higher ups than me. I just deliver it."

"Do you think you could check your bag again?" His brows furrowed, a tone of surprise in his voice.

I sucked in a deep breath and planted a smile upon my face as I took the two steps back up on his porch.

"Sure." I tugged the mail carrier bag off my shoulder and dropped it between my feet.

"Thank you," he said to the top of my head, opening his door a little more. "I'm looking for a very important document from a very serious philatelist."

"A philatelist." I tried not to smile again at the fact Lee knew the actual term for a stamp collector.

Why wouldn't he? I pondered and thumbed through what little was left in my bag. I was about to head back to the post office for my second bag of the day.

"I'm sorry. There's nothing in there. I do believe the USPS website does state the items they have photos of are coming soon, and sometimes that means a day or two." I slid my eyes over his shoulder and couldn't help but notice some moving boxes stacked up behind him. "Are you moving?"

The images of Lucas at the nursing home talking to Vivian Tillett, the director of the nursing home, made me think he'd secured a spot in the assisted-living center and was honestly going to move into the nursing area. Nah. I put the thought in my head because someone who was forgetting things didn't remember the word "philatelist."

"Heck no." He grumbled. "They'll have to carry out my dead body before I let them touch my house."

Chapter 4

My old farmhouse was on the outskirts of town and located in the county. Richard and I had made it our home, and Grady grew up here. The family dynamics were important to me when Richard and I got married. I worked hard at being a good mother to Grady and a wife to Richard, not to mention a wonderful daughter to my parents.

Every Sunday I'd fix a good homemade meal for everyone to enjoy. It wasn't uncommon in the south to have a big family supper once a week, and I continued with the tradition. It was important to our family.... or so I'd thought until a few months ago, when I found out Richard had a real relationship, not even qualifying for an affair, the entire time we were married. Or at least three-fourths of the time.

When I looked at the farmhouse now, it kind of made me sick to think I'd spent all my life making it a home that really wasn't my taste. Richard was the one who loved the deep wood tones and heavy pieces of furniture. I liked a simpler style with fewer things, but Richard didn't.

Rowena, my orange tabby rescue cat, did not come to greet me. "I'm home!" I yelled into the mud room from the garage.

I took my coat off and hung it on one of the many hooks in the mud room. It was a perfect spot for Richard's farm boots and for Grady to throw down his things when he came in from school.

Now it was just a clean spot for me to take off my shoes and hang my coat after a long day of walking. After Richard died, I'd sold all the heifers and the horses. I'd gotten rid of the farm lifestyle and let the garden pretty much go, though I did keep a few things growing.

Getting back to work was probably the best thing I did for myself. I threw myself right back into society, and now I was going out to dinner with Mac.

"There you are." I reached down and picked up Rowena when she sauntered into the mud room and rubbed up against my legs. "How was your day?" I kissed and rubbed on her a few times, listening to her purr. "Mine was the usual. Iris is stopping by to finish up some cookies." I put Rowena down and talked to her as if she understood.

She continued to rub on me and hang around my feet when I walked into the kitchen, which was good enough for me to think she was paying close attention.

"Today was fine." I switched the gas oven on so it would be preheated to the temperature Iris needed. "The town is on edge about this entire award, and you wouldn't believe how they want me to decorate my mail cart."

The headlights of Iris's car pierced through the window. Though it was still pretty early, with daylight saving time, it got dark even in the early evening hours.

"And I have a date tonight," I told Rowena, thinking I could get it out before Iris got in here.

"A date?" I heard Iris call from the mud room. "Who has a date?"

"Remind me to take away the house key from Iris," I said to Rowena, knowing Iris was standing in the door of the kitchen, trying to untie her shoes. "She is so nosy," I joked.

"Uh-huh." Iris walked in. "I'm not the only nosy one in here, and I'm not talking about you, Rowena."

"Traitor." I laughed when Rowena ran over to Iris.

Iris always baked Rowena a special cat treat and brought it for her. Rowena loved them.

"So. Who has a date?" Iris walked in and immediately rolled up her sleeves. She pulled a recipe out of her pocket and used her hands to smooth it out on the counter.

I walked over and looked at the ingredients.

"I do," I said nonchalantly walking over to the table to get the butter. I didn't refrigerate my butter. It sat in a butter dish on the table.

"What?" Iris jerked around, and her mouth flew open.

"I'm not sure whether it's a date or just another dinner together." I tried to avoid her eye contact. "Mac asked me to go help pick out some plants and flowers for the houses on Little Creek Drive, then go to eat at the new Italian place."

"And you're standing here getting ready to bake cookies." Her eyes drew up and down my body. "Looking like that?"

"I had no idea I was going to be judged tonight." I laughed and looked down at my clothes. "I was going to change out of my uniform, but the rest I thought was pretty good."

I ran my hand through my hair.

"You don't have on a stitch of makeup, and you could probably stand to take a shower." Iris rushed over, grabbed the butter dish out of my hand, and took me by the shoulders. "We are going to get you all fixed up."

"What about the bonbon cookies?" I tried to glance over my shoulder and back at the kitchen as she shoved me down the hall toward my bedroom and bathroom.

"They will be just fine." She pushed me into the bathroom at the end of the farmhouse and grabbed the doorknob. "In case you didn't know, I'm a real baker with a real shop. So I think I've got this."

"But…" I went to protest before she shut the door, then I got a glimpse of myself in the mirror. "Oh, gosh." I put both hands on top of my head. "You're right." I turned my chin to the left and then to the right, getting a good look at the fifty-year-old face staring back at me.

I barely recognized it. There were a few more wrinkles on the forehead. I ran a finger across them, hoping my finger was a magic wand and I could wipe away at least one of the lines.

Then I ran my finger down to the space between my eyebrows. It looked like a big butt crease had formed. Then I felt the dark circles under my eyes.

"I think I've let myself go since Richard died," I called from the bathroom and then turned the shower on high.

"You think?" Iris asked back in a sarcastic tone, loud enough for me to hear.

"Whatever." I groaned and got into the shower. "Maybe the hot water will melt away the wrinkles," I told Rowena, who had found her way on the bathtub ledge, a place she liked to sit when I took my showers.

I'd taken a little longer in the shower than I normally did. The water felt great, and the experience was as if the stress of the day was melting away.

"I forgot how much I liked to take baths." I wrapped myself in my long white robe and used the towel to dry a little of my hair. "I should probably take a little better care of myself."

"You've got a great figure. The walking has kept that up. And you're gorgeous. You just don't play it up." Iris was standing in my bedroom with the doors of my closet wide open. "I've picked out the green, form-fitting V-neck for you to wear." She had it tucked up under her arm, still on the hanger. "It goes so well with your skin and hair."

"What about the black pants?" I made a suggestion that was obviously not right because Iris groaned.

"Nope." She looked through the jeans. "These." She pulled out a pair of skinny jeans. "And those."

She pointed at a pair of black knee-high boots with small wedge soles.

"Oh my, I'm going to look like I'm wanting more than dinner." I knew I would be comfortable in the outfit she picked, and she was right that walking for my job did help keep me in shape. Plus I only had birthed one child, so my body did bounce back, but still. I was fifty, and I didn't want to look like some twenty-year-old going on a date, so the modest sweater was perfect.

"Mac will just love seeing you in this." She laid the outfit out on the bed. "Did you tell Grady?"

"No. I haven't talked to him." I walked into the bathroom and started to put on makeup. "He's been busy, since school is back from Christmas break."

"Is Julia okay?" Iris asked from the other room as I applied some mascara.

I stopped mid-brush up on the upper lashes.

"Why?" I had wondered the same thing.

"A feeling." Iris and her feelings made me roll my eyes.

"You also had a feeling about Mr. Macum. When I checked on him, he was as ornery as ever." I shook my head and went back to brushing on the mascara. "What is your feeling about Julia?"

"I'm not sure, but I did see her walking into the doctor's building after I made all the afternoon deliveries. I just wanted to make sure she was okay. She might have the flu. I heard it was going around." Iris walked back down the hall.

While I dried a little more of my hair, taking care so my curls wouldn't go all over the place and stay untamed, I thought about Julia and how she'd looked a little pale to me. I sure hoped Julia wasn't getting the flu. I put it in my head to make some homemade soups for her and Grady. They always appreciated when I took them food.

I quickly got my hair and makeup finished before I got dressed and then headed back down to the kitchen. Rowena was happily sitting next to Iris's feet, hoping she would drop something while she got the bonbon cookie dough on the sheet.

"Oh my goodness." Iris gasped, bringing a hand up to her chest. "If Mac Tabor doesn't get the idea that you are interested, then he's walking dead."

"Who said I was interested?" I questioned her.

"Bernadette, I know you better than I know myself." She folded her arms and smiled widely. "If you weren't interested, you'd not be looking like that."

The doorbell rang.

"Shut up," I warned. "Not a word."

Maybe she didn't say a word, but Iris did follow me to the front door, where she made kissing noises behind me.

"Since when did you have to ring the doorbell?" Iris asked Mac before he could even step inside of the house.

"Hello, Iris." Mac's eyes slid to me. A big smile formed on his face. "Wow, Bernie." He blinked a few times. "You look…"

"Doesn't she look fantastic?" Iris bounced on the tips of her toes with her hands clasped behind her.

I glared at her, feeling a bit like she was my mom, and I was about to head to the senior prom.

"Sorry." She used her finger to zip her lip. "Would you like a bonbon cookie?" she asked Mac.

"Yeah. Sounds so good." He walked past me and headed down the hall. "Did you see Walter on your delivery today?"

"I saw him at your office." I shrugged and took one of the cookies off the baking sheet. "Then again at the house you have for sale." I pointed at him. "Don't ruin your supper. I've been looking forward to a big plate of spaghetti all day."

"Then we better get going." He put a cookie in his mouth, and his eyes softened.

Was it looking at me or getting the full delicious taste of the cookie that gave him that look, I wondered. Either way, my nerves had calmed, and I felt so silly.

This was Mac. Good old friend Mac. Nothing more. At least that was what I told myself.

Chapter 5

"I'm glad to see you and Iris still bake together." Mac seemed to be making small talk when we got into his car. "She's been a really good friend to you, Bernie."

"You've been a really good friend to me," I told him.

He didn't bother looking over at me or responding. The headlights from the oncoming car broke through the windshield. I tried to stop myself from looking at Mac, but I had to see the look in his eye when I confirmed he'd been a good friend to me. There was no emotion. He just gripped the wheel and stared straight ahead.

"I guess you're having issues with Lee Macum." I decided chit-chat might be the best thing to break whatever tension was hanging between us.

"I don't get it. The man just isn't about to budge on anything. He only wants to do what he wants to do and not care about the consequences his actions have for others." By the hard tone in Mac's voice, I could tell he'd put a lot of thought into the situation with Lee. "It's not that I want him to change who he is, but he could stand to clean up his place now that we know there is a rat infestation problem."

"How do you know the rats are coming from his place?" I asked.

"Walter had Logsdon Landscape come out today, and they traced it back somehow." He shook his head. He took a left at the next street that led to Logsdon Landscape, where we were going to pick up some of the flowers. "Walter said he confronted him about it, and Lee yelled back, telling him the only rat in the town was Walter and that he only cared about money."

"Really?" I asked with a slight giggle. "Well, Lee is right."

"I know you don't like Walter and that he showed up after Richard died, but he really is passionate about his job." Mac pulled into one of the parking spots next to the greenhouse.

"Sometimes being kind is more important than a job or money." I probably should've kept my mouth shut, but I lived by the golden rule. "Do unto others," I reminded Mac.

He turned off the car and shifted his body slightly towards me. He lifted his hand and put it on top of mine, which was resting on the console between us.

"That's why you're a good person and you deserve so much happiness." His words struck me as odd. Was he trying to tell me something *without* telling me something?

Before I could question him, he got out of the car and ran over to my side to open the door.

"Why, Mac Tabor, have you been taking southern gentleman classes?" I lifted my hand to my chest and did my best impression of Scarlett O'Hara.

"Oh for you, my dear." He tried his best Rhett Butler and did a little bow.

Both of us laughed and headed toward the lit-up

greenhouse, where we found a few of the Logsdon employees and the owner, Amy Logsdon.

"Hey, you two." She looked up from the small potted plant she was trimming. "Happy New Year."

"Yeah, you too." I tried not to be too embarrassed when I looked at her because it wasn't long ago that I'd pegged her for a murderer. "I bet you're going crazy."

"With Carla or trying to get more flowers in stock?" she asked with a grin.

"Both," I commented.

"I'm not complaining. Every year about this time, I'm busying trying to recover from the holidays, and I have time to do that. Plus, the income is generally slow, so I'm kind of happy with the uptake in business, but it comes with long hours." Amy did a couple of more snips before she looked at it one more time and then motioned for one of the workers to take it away.

She wiped her hands down her apron.

"What can I do for you two tonight?" she asked and looked between Mac and me.

"I'm here looking for something that'll take away from Lee's place." Mac didn't try to hold back.

"I heard it's a mess over there. And the rats." She gasped and shook her head. "Walter had come by earlier today to look, too, but Mac, I just don't have anything that'll make a world of difference when you got an eyesore from him. Or that will get rid of rats that quickly. He needs a spray, and I tried calling him, but there was no answer."

Mac looked around and was very quiet, like he was pondering what Amy had told him. I gave her a slight shrug.

"I bet you're happy you don't have to worry about getting the farm all dolled up for this." Amy was right. I was happy.

"That doesn't leave me exempt from Carla." I still couldn't believe she gave me the kit to decorate my cart, and I told Amy about it.

"Oh my goodness, she's too much." Amy sucked in a deep breath then glanced over my shoulder at Mac.

I turned around to see that he had a flowering plant in each hand.

"What about these?" he looked at me and asked.

"Those are winter jasmine. They can bloom in a variety of colors, but they won't shield anyone's eyes from Lee's house." I wasn't sure how many times Amy would say that until Mac heard her, but he went ahead and bought ten of them in various colors and paid to have them delivered.

"Can I get them planted along the fence on both sides of the house that's for sale?" He pulled out his wallet and took out a stack of cash, casually counting out the hundreds. "Do you like them?" He looked at me.

"They are pretty." I wasn't too much on flowers since they did die in the winter, and no matter how much Carla wanted to pull it off that Sugar Creek Gap was in full spring, it wasn't.

I watched the weather closely and also read the *Farmers' Almanac*, which told me it was going to be a late spring. That meant we could have a frost at any time, and I hated to see Mac waste his money on something that wasn't going to last. But I kept my mouth shut. It wasn't my place.

"Then I'll take the same amount for the other house I'm rehabbing on Little Creek Road." Mac pulled out another stack of cash.

"What are you doing with that house after you're finished working on it?" Amy asked and rang up his purchase.

"Let's just get the house I've got listed with Walter sold

before I can make any decisions on it." Mac handed her a stack of cash.

"The way Walter operates, he'd stop at nothing to get your place sold and make a buck." Amy was right, and it was the exact same thing I'd been saying about Walter for a good ten years now, but again, I kept my mouth shut.

"Oh, Bernadette." Amy stopped me shy of the door. When I turned around and made eye contact, she said, "I'll be sure to look out for your twinkling mail cart."

We both laughed.

"What was she talking about?" Mac asked on our way to the car.

Both of us had a good laugh when I told him about it on our drive to the new Italian restaurant.

"Paisanos." I read the name of the restaurant out loud. "You can't get more Italian than that."

"From what I hear, you have to go to Italy to get anywhere near this good." He had put his hand on the small of my back as we walked into the restaurant.

It was unlike any restaurant in Sugar Creek Gap, and I had to wonder if it would make it. Only the mom-and-pop diners were big hits around here, but I'd love to see more growth in our town.

The lighting was dim. It sort of reminded me of old Hollywood or what I thought old Hollywood was like. There were tables all around the perimeter of the room, with a few more located in the middle. The white table-cloths made the atmosphere feel very romantic, as did the lit candles in the red votives in the center of the table. A wine chiller stand was also located at each table.

"Reservation for Tabor," Mac held up two fingers and told the hostess.

"Fancy." I gave him a big-eyed look. "What's the occasion?"

Boy… did I ask a loaded question with an answer I wasn't prepared for.

"You're special." His hand, which was flat on my back, was now giving me a little scratch.

I gulped.

"Right this way," the hostess said just in time for me to take a few steps and get out of my head, which was saying, *Oh crap, oh crap.*

Was this a real date? Was this…

"First time here?" the hostess asked.

"Yes." Mac looked at her and then walked over to my chair. He pulled it out for me.

I gulped. My mouth and lips were dry. The water on the table couldn't've been poured fast enough.

"Let me give you a few suggestions on wine." The hostess's words ran together as I gulped down the water. "And some dinner options."

She told us the specials, and we picked the spaghetti, figuring it had to be their best dish.

When she walked away, I noticed Mac looking at me.

"I don't think I've ever seen you drink water so fast." There was an amused look on his face with a little twinkle in his eye that told me he knew I was nervous.

"Tasting the batter from the bonbon cookies really has me parched," I lied and picked up the water carafe to refill my glass.

"Are you sure that's it?" he asked.

"Mm-hhmm," I ho-hummed while taking another gulp of water.

"Mac. Bernadette." Luke Macum interrupted us, and I couldn't've been more thrilled to see him. "Mac, I must apologize for my uncle's behavior."

"Oh no. He owns the house. It's his property." Mac's reaction to Luke's question didn't really surprise me.

Though I knew Mac thought differently, he wasn't one to make waves, and he just went with it.

"That's funny." Luke shot Mac a perplexed look. "My uncle called me saying how Walter Ward and Carla were driving him crazy about how bad his property looked. He rambled on and on about how much the stuff meant to him, but when I asked why it meant so much"—Luke frowned and looked down at his hands—"he couldn't remember."

"Oh no." I couldn't stop the words from coming out of my mouth. "Luke, I'm sorry, and I don't mean to overstep, but I did overhear you talking to Vivian Tillett at the nursing home this morning. Were you talking about Lee?"

"I'm afraid he's not as sharp as he used to be." Luke's eyes dipped. "I'm his only relative here, and I try to stop in once a week, if not more, but he doesn't let me through the door. Today"—his voice cracked—"I went over there after he called me, and that was when I noticed it'd gotten worse. He's got boxes piled high from his hoarding. There's nothing in most of them, but he won't throw them away. I even had to go back and spray for bugs, though he didn't know what I was doing."

"I sure hate to hear that." I felt a pain in my heart. "I've enjoyed taking stamps to him over the years."

"He always said how kind you are to him. In fact, I think you're the only person he likes around here," Luke said jokingly, but I knew it wasn't a joke.

"What about Buster? Is he being taken care of?" I asked, feeling desperately sorry for the pooch if he wasn't getting proper care.

"Somehow he still remembers to take care of Buster." Luke smiled. "It's not that he's forgetful all the time. It's some of the time. Then the hoarding. It's not helping." He turned to Mac. "Again, I'm sorry. Walter took me out to breakfast at the Wallflower, and he really wanted me to do something. Apparently my uncle's home isn't helping his bottom dollar to sell your house. But I can't just rip him out of the house in the next few days just so Carla can win some beautification award before she retires."

"No problem." Mac stood up and put his hand out for Luke to shake. "I understand. We only want the best for Lee." Mac gestured between him and me.

What was that? We?

Luke said his goodbyes when the hostess brought our food, and Mac sat back down.

"That was kind of you." I reached for the wine glass, needing a little more than water. "And to include me in the we." I found some sort of courage to be vocal.

"You know when I told you how Iris has been a really good friend to you, and you said how I've been a really good friend to you?" Mac asked. The candles between us flickered, making it hard for me to see the look in his eyes that would tell me where his questioning would be going.

"Mmhmmm." I curled the noodles around the tines on my fork like people did in the movies, trying to be a little more ladylike.

"I want to be more than a friend to you, Bernadette." Mac put his hand on top of mine. Either the warmth of his hand or the words he said put my head and heart into a tailspin.

Chapter 6

The evening with Mac ended with him dropping me off at the farmhouse. We had no dramatic ending. Not that I was looking for a kiss or even a "That was great," but when he'd told me he wanted to be more than friends, I was figuring on some sort of romantic gesture at the end of the night.

Even Rowena agreed with me when I told her about it as I was getting ready for bed. Or at least she appeared to be interested. Or... she could've been interested in the leftover chicken leg that I was eating while changing into my pajamas. Either way, the poor baby had to hear my woes. When I couldn't fall asleep so quickly, I used the rest of the leftover chicken I had to make the soup for Julia and Grady.

I didn't bother calling Iris because I knew she'd call me in the morning, dying to know the details. And I was right.

"More than friends? Is that what he said?" Iris asked from the other end of the phone. "Then no kiss? No nothing?"

"Mmm-hhmmm," I ho-hummed on my way into the post office, where I was getting an early jump on the day. Most times when I tried to get the mail delivered earlier than usual, it backfired. Something always popped up. Julia was on my mind, and I wanted to be sure to get those soups over to her. I also made a note to pick up something special from Leotta at Social Knitwork, since Julia had been spending some time there. A small gift always paired well with food. And it gave me a check in the awesome mother-in-law category.

"Not even a lean over?" Iris referred to Mac not trying to lean over the console to kiss me.

"Not even a lean over," I confirmed. "Listen, I'm at the post office and going to get a jump on things. When you told me you saw Julia going into the doctor's building, it got me a little concerned she was getting the flu. When I couldn't sleep after the no-kiss and I-want-to-be-more-than-friends thing…" I hesitated when I noticed someone rush by the post office door from the outside.

"You there?" Iris asked.

I looked out the glass plate door. Nothing was there.

"Yeah. I'm fine. Just at work, and like I said, I want to get a jump on things so I can drop off the soup I made because I couldn't sleep." I took one more look outside, where the LLVs were, but I saw nothing and no one.

"That's sweet." Iris continued to talk. "Say, did you and Mac talk about Lee Macum at all? I still have a funny feeling about him."

"Not that I have a lot of time, but we did see Luke at the restaurant. He did confirm that Lee had been a little more forgetful." It was so sad to watch my customers get elderly. "It's a shame. I'm going to be sure to give him extra attention while he's still living in the house on Little Creek."

"He's moving?" Iris asked. "You know, I can totally see you living in that house."

"I don't think so." I laughed as I walked into the sorting room to pick up my first loop bag, which Monica Reed had already sorted for me. "Thank you," I mouthed to Monica and headed back the way I'd come.

"That is a great idea. You're nuts. You should ask him." Iris made it sound as if it were already a done deal.

"It's not even for sale." I pushed the door open to walk outside. "Besides, if I wanted to live on Little Creek Road, I could buy one of Mac's houses."

"I don't know." Iris was now sounding odd.

"You need another cup of coffee." I sighed and jerked my head when I noticed something run past the side of the post office parking lot. "You sound delirious. Listen…" I craned my neck to see what the shadow was that was moving around. "I've got to go. Call you later."

If I didn't hang up right then, it would give Iris a small window of opportunity to ask another question, keeping me on the phone.

"Who's there?" I stopped and called out when I heard some sort of jingling. "We have cameras back here, so if you're trying to steal one of the LLVs, well, first off they are crap, and secondly…"

The shadow moved and showed itself. The lights in the parking lot shined down.

"Buster?" I asked when I noticed it was a dog that certainly looked a lot like Lee's dog Buster. "Bussssster. Here, boy."

He twisted his head and started to wag his tail when I called out to him, so I began to call him more.

"Come here, sweet boy." I tugged a dog treat out of the pocket of my coat and bent down to greet him when he rushed over. "What on earth are you doing over here?"

He gobbled up the treat and then a couple more.

Then it dawned on me.

"Oh, buddy," I groaned, my heart hurt. "Did your daddy let you out and forget about you?" I sighed and pushed myself up to stand. "The first loop is going to have to wait." I smiled at him He was looking up at me with those big brown eyes and wagging his tail like I was the best thing he'd seen all night. "Come on." I patted my leg. "Let's get you home."

Instead of taking the long way down Main Street, left on Short, and then a left on Little Creek, I had decided to take the short cut between the Sugar Creek Gap Veterinarian Clinic and Social Knitwork, which were located right across the street from the post office. I took that path by way of the foot bridge that crossed over Little Creek and directly in front of Lee's home.

On our way over the bridge, I asked Buster, "Did you give my duck a hard time?" There, I heard the water in the creek moving from my duck friend paddling underneath the bridge, probably away from the dog.

Buster didn't obviously answer, but the wag of his tail and the mud on his feet told me he had not been very nice to my friend. I'd be sure to make it up to the duck when I met him at our usual time and at the other end of the street with a spectacular treat from the Wallflower Diner.

Buster rushed across the street and through the open gate, which I found to be particularly odd. I'd never seen Lee's gate open in the ten years I'd delivered his mail. When Buster disappeared into the house, I knew something had to be horribly wrong. I knew for sure Lee didn't leave his door open.

The inside lights were on, but when I pushed open the door a little more with the toe of my shoe, the shadows from all the piled-up boxes made it so dim and dreary.

"Mr. Macum?" I called into the house without stepping in. I waited for a few seconds to see if I could hear him. "Lee?" I called again, thinking he was not answering since he'd insisted I call him Lee. That wouldn't be out of his character.

There was still no answer.

"I bet he can't hear from all these boxes in the way." I took one step inside. "Lee!" I yelled a couple of times.

I heard a few whimpers that sounded a lot like Buster and not a human.

"Lee, I'm coming in," I warned like it was going to make him answer me. "It's Bernadette, your mail carrier." I talked as if we were playing some sort of game. I weaved around the boxes, having to turn around a few times at various dead ends. "Buster was at the post office, and I just thought I'd bring him home."

The whimpering got a little louder as I made my way through the maze of boxes.

"This is gross," I muttered to myself and decided I'd call Luke about this when I'd found Lee safe and sound. "How does anyone live like this?" I let out a deep sigh.

Buster's whimper got a little louder which made me think I was getting closer. The closer I got, the more I started to hear a TV, which made me feel somewhat better. Lee had to be asleep in front of the television, and Buster probably wanted to eat.

At least, that was what I told myself.

"Lee?" My eyes focused on a pair of shoes, sticking straight up in the air, with… legs attached. The television played the morning news, and Buster was sitting next to the feet. "Lee?" I gulped and moved around the stack of boxes that covered my full view of what once was probably the living room of his home.

There, in plain view, was Lee, lying face up in the

middle of the only open floorspace. His eyes were open, and his hand was outstretched in a strange open space with boxes built up around it as if something once there was now gone. Kind of like that Jenga game my family loved to play. One wrong move and they would all come tumbling down.

"Lee?" My voice cracked. My eyes stung with the tears that were starting to collect. "Lee? Please tell me you're alive." I couldn't bring my focus off the stamp Lee had in his open palm. It was the stamp I'd given him yesterday from my dad.

My head dipped when I noticed no movement from Lee, and my heart sank when Buster licked his beloved owner's cold face.

Chapter 7

I immediately left the house and maneuvered my way back out the door to call the sheriff's department. I didn't want to disturb anything, and I left Buster in there, but he came out a few minutes later.

I gave the poor guy some more treats because I didn't know how long he'd been without food or water. It wasn't like I was going to go in there to find him some food, so I continued to give him what I had as we waited on steps of Lee's front porch for a deputy to show up, which didn't take long since the department was located one street over on Main Street.

"Hey, Bernadette." Sheriff Angela Hafley herself had come.

"Angie, I'm surprised to see you here." Not that she didn't have a right, but when people died of what appeared to be a heart attack, such as in Lee's case, the sheriff's office generally sent a deputy and the coroner.

"We are the only ones in the office this early." She reached out her hand for Buster to sniff and then patted him on the head. "I got the information from dispatch that you found the dog at the post office and walked over to bring him home. When you noticed the door was open, you went in?"

"Yes." I stood up on the step. The deputy with her walked into the house, leaving her there with me. "First Lee's gate was open, which is odd. Then the door of the house was cracked, and Buster ran in."

"Why is it odd the gate was open?" She looked back over her shoulder at the gate.

"Lee never left that gate unlatched. He was very private and didn't want people coming on his property." I snorted in a bit of sadness when I remembered Carla trying to get in his gate and him drawing back his curtains. "And he'd never leave his door open."

"Why is that?" Angie asked me with a curious eye before she looked up at the deputy who was now standing in Lee's doorway.

I looked back. He shook his head, frowning with a sadness in his eyes. I noticed her give him a slight nod, and some sort of body language went on between them before the officer disappeared back into the house.

"I'm sorry. Why is it odd?" Angela didn't miss a beat as she reminded me of the question she wanted me to answer.

"Again, in the last ten years, when I've needed to hand him something, he would take forever unlocking all the chains and locks he had on his door."

Then I suddenly remembered what Luke had told me last night.

"Though I guess he was getting forgetful." A long deep sigh escaped me.

"How do you know that?" Angie was darting me with questions that made me pause. "Not that I'm not saying he's died of natural causes, but I can't help but think about all the grief I've been getting from people in the community who wanted me to arrest him for not keeping his property in pristine condition for various reasons."

She didn't have to tell me who she was talking about. I knew she meant Carla and Walter. I didn't say a word.

About that time, Jigs Baker, the coroner and funeral home director, showed up with his hearse. And the SPCA van pulled up right behind him.

"What's going on?" I asked, more about the SPCA van than anything, and put my hand on Buster's head.

"We need to take Lee Macum to the morgue and make sure he died of a heart attack." Angie avoided looking at me. She knew I was an animal lover, and there was no way I'd ever let her take Buster to the dog pound.

"I mean with the SPCA." I grabbed Buster by the collar. "You're going to have to use that gun on me to get my grip from around his collar."

"Don't be ridiculous, Bernadette." She shifted to the right, and her head followed. "If you'll excuse me, we need to call Luke and get this all cleared up."

"Listen, Angie." I talked to her like the friends we once had been, but we were not so close anymore. "Let me get Buster looked at by Doc Olson."

Angie huffed and then sucked in a breath and watched the SPCA employee walk by with one of those loop catchers.

"Please. Buster isn't a bad dog. He's good," I begged, keeping my eye on the SPCA worker. "I'm even a mail carrier. Most dogs hate me. Go get Carl Hirth's dog. It never lets me deliver the mail." I was on edge, and my nerves made me shake. Buster was sitting on the front porch just looking out over his domain, and when the SPCA employee approached him, Buster's tail started to wag.

"Calm down, Bernadette." Angie walked up to the SPCA employee and must have whispered something about me because they both turned and looked at me.

When he turned and walked back to his truck, I smiled at Angie, almost feeling a sense of compassion from her.

"Thank you." I bit my lip to try not to cry.

"If the dog comes back with rabies or something, then we will deal with it. Tell Doc Olson to send me the blood work and any other tests he might be doing." Angie's eyes shifted past me.

"Oh dear, oh dear." Millie Barnes hurried through Lee's gate, closely followed by Gertrude, Ruby and Harriette. "What is all this about? Did Buster bite you?"

Millie and the front porch ladies didn't give two iotas that Angie was there. They just shoved right past her.

"I knew that dog was going to get someone one day." Gertrude looked at Millie and nodded, and they all followed.

"Buster isn't going to bite anyone," I said through gritted teeth, fully aware Angie's brows were lifted.

About that time the church cart with Lee's body was trying to burst through the door, and Jigs Baker was on the other end, trying to push it through. The cart was stuck on the other side of the threshold. The more Jigs pushed, the more I could see the white sheet that covered Lee's body falling to the side.

"The sheet is caught." I tried to get it out, but the sheet fell completely off, Lee's right hand flung down off the church cart, and the front porch ladies got a full view of what was really happening.

"Oh," Ruby Dean gasped right before she went down. I mean plumb passed out, flat out on the ground.

"Ruby!" The women rushed down to Ruby's side.

Angie pushed past them to help Jigs get the church cart

going again, and I grabbed Buster's collar so he wouldn't start running around. That was the last thing I needed.

"Don't just stand there, Bernie. Help us," Harriette instructed me.

"I'm not a paramedic. What do you want me to do?" I blinked a few times. "I guess just sit with her?"

I know my words and my unwillingness to help stung Harriette, but it wasn't that I was unwilling. I just didn't want to get in the way. Angie had already called one of the EMTs who'd showed up after Jigs to come help Ruby. He'd already had her sitting up. Though she was groggier and talking out of her head, she was alive and had just passed out.

"What happened?" Harriette was the youngest and the ringleader of her little group of four.

"I don't really know. Heart attack?" I questioned what appeared to be the most logical explanation.

"Or murder?" Harriette's eyes darkened, and she glanced over her shoulder just as Carla had pulled up in her car to the curb right in front of Lee's house.

"Murder, huh?" *Angie's ears are trained to hear everything*, I groaned inwardly.

"Look at Carla." Harriette nodded with her chin toward Carla's car. "She's been harassing the man for weeks about his house and this stupid pretty award or whatever the heck it is."

"That's right," Gertrude interrupted. "She's been down here knocking on his door, delivering the fines from the city herself." She gave a hard nod.

"She doesn't even work for the city." Harriette and Gertrude spilled the beans about poor Carla.

"And just how do you think she murdered him?" Angie asked a great question because trust me, there were no signs of visible murder.

Lee had no bloodstains on him. He had his eyes open, and he sure didn't look like he'd been strangled—not that I was an expert. I'd only been involved in one other murder....

Angie looked very amused by the banter between the two women. She finally stopped them from being the Jessica Fletcher of Sugar Creek Gap.

"Ladies, I really appreciate all of this information, but we are in the preliminary facts of the Lee's death. There were no visible signs of murder, but trust me, Jigs will do his job as coroner and find out the exact cause of death." Angie wasn't going to give any more information. I'd seen this switch of her personality before. "How is Millie?" Angie asked the EMT.

"Honey, she'll be fine." Harriette waved off any sort of concern. "She's just wound tighter than a girdle at the Baptist church potluck."

Then Harriette did something very non-Harriette. She gestured for Ruby and Gertrude to help her with Millie, and then they all headed back toward their houses. It was definitely out of Harriette's character not to stick around, so it made me wonder what she was hiding. She was absolutely hiding something.

"What?" Angie asked, bringing me back to looking at her.

"What?" I asked.

"Bernadette, I know that look in your eye. You're thinking something. What is it?" She could ask all she wanted, but I wasn't going to say anything about my suspicion of Harriette hiding something.

"I'm just thinking you should go see what Carla wants." I continued to hold tight to Buster. "And you probably want to call Luke."

"Thank you for doing my job, but we've already called

Luke." Angie's face pinched.

Just as she said his name, Luke drove up. He jumped out of his car.

"What on earth?" He had a blank look on his face. His hair was messed up, and he still wore his blue-striped pajama pants and UGG house slippers. He noticed Jigs putting the church cart in the hearse. I watched Luke's body language and expression when he was able to look under the sheet at Lee. Luke ran away from us, his brown overcoat flapping behind him.

"This is terrible," I whispered under my breath.

"It never gets any easier." Angie's warm palm she planted on my arm was somewhat comforting. "Anyway, thank you for calling. I'm sure Luke appreciates how kind you have been to Lee all these years."

That was odd. Why was Angie apologizing to me? It seemed a little more personal than I thought it should be.

"Yeah. No problem." I gave her a sideways glance. Buster must've been tired of me holding on to him. He wiggled free and went to the side yard to do some business.

"Why don't you head on out?" she suggested when Luke was walking back. "I'd like to talk to Luke alone." She straightened her shoulders and took what I liked to call the cop stance—hands on her utility belt, legs spread apart, and her face stern. "I'll let you know if we need to get an official statement from you."

"Official statement?" Luke overheard Angie. "Ang, what's going on? Was my uncle murdered?"

"Why would you think that?" I asked him, thinking it was awfully strange of him to even think such a way.

"There's all this going on." He gestured to all the hubbub. He looked back at Carla's car when she drove off. "Why is Carla here?"

"Luke…" Angie had a more loving tone to her voice.

"I'm sure over ninety-nine percent of the citizens in this town have police scanners. You know how they rubberneck."

"Or chase ambulances." I couldn't help but point out that Walter Ward had pulled his car up in front of the hearse and was getting out.

My eyes narrowed as I watched him walk up. He had his own eyes on Luke.

"Excuse me." Luke gave us the one finger and met Walter halfway up the sidewalk inside the yard.

"I'll keep you posted about Buster," I told Angie and decided it was time for me to go. Something felt off here. I wasn't sure what it was, but it did.

My phone rang deep in my mail carrier bag. As I searched for the phone, I passed Walter and Luke talking in hushed voices on my way over to grab Buster.

"I told you I'd call you," I overheard Luke say to Walter in a scorned tone.

"I figured something changed," Walter responded.

"Come on, Buster." I patted my leg with one hand and grabbed the phone with the other, taking it out of the bag. "Hey, Iris."

"Hey, Iris?" A quiet snort came from the back of her throat through the phone. "All you have to say is 'Hey, Iris'? Or 'Oh my God, Iris, you were right about your feelings. Something awful happened to Lee Macum…'" She paused. "'Like death'!"

Chapter 8

On my way up Little Creek Road with Buster, I assured Iris her timing was odd but also that Lee had appeared to have died of natural causes. Still, she wanted me to be very aware that her feeling was somewhat spot on when she knew I was a skeptic of her self-proclaimed talent. I did thank her for the heads up, though it would've been nice to have gotten her prediction right before it actually happened and not the day of. Either way, Lee was dead, and I told her I'd let her know of any of the gossip I was sure to encounter today.

"Here, Buster!" I called Buster's name when I unlatched Mac's gate. Buster happily followed me into Mac's yard, where he found a lot of new smells to keep him occupied while I took a shot at begging Mac to take Buster to the vet for me.

"I thought I heard someone trespassing." Mac stood on the other side of his screen door.

Some screen, I thought with an inwardly sigh when the screen didn't shield Mac's toned bare chest from my eyes.

"Let me get you one," Mac said.

"One what?" I gulped. One toned bicep? Two?

"You're staring at my coffee cup." *He saw me staring?* I blushed. "Weren't you?"

"I'm sorry." I shook my head. "I was trying to collect my thoughts."

"Buster, what are you doing in my yard." Mac unlocked the screen door and walked out in his bare feet and black pajama pants, no shirt.

"Actually," I put my hands together in pray pose. "We are here to ask for a favor. You see, I found Lee dead in his home."

I watched Mac's face go from surprised to confused to just plain blank.

"I'm sorry. Did you say dead?" He leaned a little forward towards me and looked down the street where everyone was still gathered in front of Lee's house.

His smell...that smell that always had been so appealing to me even when Richard was alive made my heart skip a few beats.

Okay! I'll be more than friends! I wanted to yell so bad.

"I've got to get dressed." He turned to hurry back into his house. "You had me all tuckered out last night when I got home and I missed my alarm. Every time I take my time going into the office, I miss out on something."

"Let me assure you that you missed out on nothing. Buster was running around the post office," My mind literally just heard how he said I tuckered him out. "Tuckered you out?"

He turned around, giving me a half smile.

"Sometimes I wonder where your mind goes." He reached out with his free hand and touched my temple. "You Bernadette, you confuse me sometimes." He winked.

I gulped, again. "What were you saying about Buster?"

"He was running around the post office this morning,

64

and I decided to take him home. That was when I found Lee's door open, and I called out to him. I went inside and found him dead." I made sure to keep my eyes on Mac's face and not any other body part.

"That's awful. I can't believe he's dead." He shook his head.

"And Angie was going to send Buster to the SPCA, but I begged her to let me take him to Doc Olson—only I'm short on time. I don't have any mail in my bag because I figured I was going to drop Buster off and then head straight back to the post office."

"You want me to take him?" Mac's eyes softened, and he looked over at Buster, who was still sniffing every single piece of grass in the yard. "No problem. Anything for you."

"I have no idea how to thank you." My breath caught in my throat.

"How about cooking me dinner tonight at your house?" He wasn't shy, was he?

"Yeah." I blinked a few times. "Sure."

Then I thought of the million little things like how dirty my house was and how I needed to run to the grocery store, not to mention what on earth I was going to cook for him.

"Great." He reached out and put his hand on my arm. "I hope I didn't overstep last night when I suggest we be more than friends. It's just that we are two fifty-somethings that need companionship, and I find it so easy to be with you. I was up all night thinking about how stupid I sounded. I know we aren't teenagers anymore, but you…"

"It's fine." I couldn't do this talk at this very moment. "I like you too."

Oh my God, "I like you too"? Ugh. Now I felt really stupid.

"We can talk about it later." He squeezed my arm before he let go. "I'll bring the wine."

"Great," I said, only I knew I would need something much stronger than wine. "Buster," I called to the pup, and he ran up on the front porch. "You be a good boy for Mac."

Mac opened the door wider. Buster took the cue and ran in.

"I'm sure we are going to be just fine." He gave me that million-dollar smile one more time before he disappeared into the house.

I took a lot of deep breaths on my way back to the post office to clear my head of anything involving Mac Tabor. If one thing was for sure, he sent me into a tailspin that would last all day if I let it. I hated to even think it, but Lee's death was gladly taking over the mental space that thoughts of Mac had occupied because everyone on my route was talking about it. Not only did that help take my mind off my "companionship," as Mac had labeled it, but it also got me off the hook of being late to deliver the mail. Even the shop owners and my parents didn't have time to properly talk to me. They were all caught up in who was going to fix what for Lee's repass.

The repass. I'd not even thought about that. I was sure he was going to have his funeral in the Sugar Creek Gap Baptist Church, so when I went there to deliver the mail, I knocked on Brother Don's office door.

"Bernadette, come in." Brother Don was the preacher and had been for years. He'd even married me and Richard. That was how long I'd known him.

"Hi." I greeted him back and took the invitation to come into his office. "I was wondering if you've gotten any sort of timeline for when Lee Macum's funeral will be?"

"Oh." Brother Don's office chair squeaked when he

eased back, his hand popped up like a tent on his belly. "Such an unfortunate event. You know, Lee hadn't been in church for years, and he was on my list to go see today."

"Really? That's a coincidence." I wondered if he, too, had the self-proclaimed gift.

"Not really. Luke, as you know, is a very big contributor to the church, and well, let's just say he loves—loved"— Brother Don corrected himself—"his uncle very much and cared for his well-being."

"Yes." I wondered what that meant but shoved it in the back of my head. "Very sad. But I was asking since I was here to deliver your mail." I reached down in my bag and took out the taco-shaped mismatched envelopes for the church I'd bound with a rubber band. Then I handed him the mail over his desk. "Because I need to take off work. The sooner, the better."

"Unfortunately, Lee didn't have those details. They are doing an autopsy to make sure Lee died of a heart attack." A somber look crossed over Brother Don's eyes. "I'm sure he's through those pearly gates," he assured me like I was asking where Lee had moved on to.

"I'm sure he is." I stood up and said my goodbyes.

Normally, I'd have thought this was a waste of time and I'd have gotten farther along on my route if I'd not stopped to talk, but I couldn't get the idea out of my head that Luke had already asked Brother Don to go see Lee. Then again, as Brother Don mentioned, Luke did and had really taken extra effort to make sure Lee was taken care of.

No matter what, Lee was dead, and Buster was still at Doc Olson's clinic. I'd not heard from her, and I wondered how things were going. Instead of going back to the post office to leave my mail bag for the night, I walked down Main Street and carefully crossed over to the other side, where the veterinarian clinic was located. I decided to pop my head in and suddenly Carla's car zoomed past me.

I jumped up on the sidewalk, narrowly preventing her from clipping my leg. She and her car came to an abrupt stop, I stopped wondering if she was going to jump out and ask me about Lee. Well, I had a few questions for her myself.

But I didn't have to worry about her. She jumped out of the car with her spray bottle in hand and squirted the lonely weed growing up between the crack of the curb and the pavement. Then she jumped right back in her car and zoomed off to what I figured was more weed hunting.

Poor weeds. They didn't stand a chance from Carla and that bottle of poisonous weed killer.

"Bernie, you just about missed me." Doc Jeanine Olson was hanging up her white lab coat on the coat tree just inside the small Sugar Creek Gap Veterinarian Clinic. "I told Kayla to let you know Buster is in great shape. Poor guy." Her lips turned down. "Anyways, I've got to go. I've got to go to the beautification meeting and tell them they need to put a stop to Carla and her poison. I've had so many sick animals in here from her just stopping wherever she feels and spraying. She doesn't care at all that she's trespassing into people's yards and making their pets sick when they go outside."

"Oh no. I hate to hear that." I let go of a deep sigh but perked up when Kayla brought Buster out from the other room. "I'm so glad to hear you're fine."

"As fine as he can be." Doc Olson tugged on her jacket. "He might have some grieving about Lee, so don't be worried if he's not eating his full amount."

"Full amount? Grieving? Not eating?" I continued to ask all sorts of questions that I'd not even thought out.

"Yes. You're his new owner, so I figured you had all the

particulars about his diet and exercise." I guess she could see the look on my face. "Don't worry." She leaned around me. "Kayla, please give Bernadette a copy of Buster's file and history. We want him to stay healthy. Just like you take care of Rowena." She patted me and headed out the door.

"I'll be just a minute," Kayla assured me, waving the manila folder in front of her. She disappeared into the room behind the desk.

"How are you, Buster?" I asked him. He looked up at me with those big brown eyes. Instantly my heart dropped. He had no idea how his life was about to change. There was no way I could keep him. I was never home during the day, and that was why I'd gotten Rowena.

Rowena was a rescue cat, and she didn't need all the attention a dog did, which was why I didn't have one. It wouldn't be fair to the dog to have to sit there all day and hold his business or worse… potty in the house. If I lived in town, maybe, but I didn't. I lived in the country in an old farmhouse. Perfect for a cat.

"Here you go." Kayla walked out, extending a stack of papers. "He's due for his annual checkup in two weeks. Do you want me to go ahead and make the appointment for you?"

"I'll let the new owners do that." I took the papers from her.

"New owners? I thought…" A lightbulb seemed to go off in her head. Her demeanor turned suddenly. Her face grew still, and her right brow rose slightly.

She was judging me. I could see her judging me.

"I'm never home." I pointed to the mail bag hoisted across my body. "It wouldn't be fair to Buster for him to sit in the house all day."

I had no idea why I was explaining this much. She put me on the spot.

"I'm sorry. Doc Olson and I assumed you were taking him, since you're listed on the emergency contact form." Her face didn't twitch. It didn't even move a tiny bit. She just stared. Judging me.

"I'm the emergency contact?" My jaw dropped.

"Mmm-hhhhmm." Kayla tapped the air towards me with her index finger. "Right there in the first page."

My eyes scanned down the page, and right there in Lee's handwriting—and I knew his chicken scratch from the mail he sent out—were my name and phone number. How did he get my phone number?

"How much do I owe?" I decided to let this sink in. I wasn't thinking clearly.

"Nothing. Mac Tabor gave us his credit card." Kayla shrugged, still had that judging eye on me. "If you don't find a home for Buster, I'm sure he won't live long at the shelter."

"What?" I gasped.

"Not that he'd be put to sleep." Kayla rolled her eyes at me. "He'll be first to get adopted, so don't feel too bad if you don't take him. Even though that's clearly what Lee intended. But who am I to judge?"

My eyes lowered. *Yeah, who are you to judge? Even though you did.* Sometimes it was just best to keep my mouth shut. At least, my mom always said, "*If you can't say nothing good, don't say nothin' at all.*" Clearly, Kayla wasn't southern. Or she'd know better.

"Tell Doc Olson thank you." I patted my leg. "Let's go, Buster. I bet you're hungry. And I know just the place to go."

"Ummm…" Kayla stopped me with a happy smirk on her face. "If you read his chart, you'll see Buster is on a diet. He could stand to lose a few pounds."

With a smile planted on my face, I nodded and took Buster right on out the door.

"Need to lose weight?" I scoffed at her words. "We can all stand to lose a few pounds, can't we? But not today."

We headed up Main Street and passed by Social Knitwork and Tranquility Wellness before we made it to the diner. The smell of fresh cornbread and Mom's bean soup greeted my nose before she greeted me.

"Hey, honey!" Mom waved the dish towel from the pass-through window when she noticed me. "Buster." Mom's eyes grew big, and she darted out of the kitchen.

"Hi, mom." I tried to greet her with a hug, but she went straight for pup kisses from Buster.

"Buster, I'm so sorry, you sweet baby boy." Mom's baby talk made me grin. She was always a lover of animals and I was sure I'd gotten the trait from her. "Honey, did you find him a home?"

"I haven't tried. I just figured I'd take him home with me tonight and on my route tomorrow see if anyone would like a good dog for a pet." Mom finally hugged me.

The diner was filled with the regulars who came on bean soup night. Mom made the best bean soup, and when you added in her fried cornbread and some chopped-up onion… your belly sang happy tunes.

"Can I rustle him up something good for him?" she asked. "I already have something for Rowena." She turned and headed back towards the kitchen.

Whether or not I agreed that Buster could have something, she was going to make him something anyway.

"I'm going to run upstairs and drop off some homemade chicken soup for Grady and Julia," I told her. "Come on, Buster."

Buster followed me over to the door on the far-right

side of the diner, which led up to the one-bedroom apartment upstairs.

The steps were steep and just big enough for one person to go up at a time. They didn't lead right into the apartment. A hallway and a storage room were up there as well. Mom and Dad used that room mostly for paper products and maybe some legal documentation.

Buster sniffed his way to the apartment door.

"You knew someone is in there." I was learning new things about my little buddy. "You're a smart dog."

The door whipped open before I could even knock.

"Mom." Grady had a wide-eyed look of surprise on his face. "What are you doing here?"

"I came bearing gifts." I went to dig down into my mail carrier bag to grab the soup.

"If you're trying to give us Buster, we are in no way needing a pet right now." Grady bent down and patted Buster.

"That would be a no. I would never try to give you a pet without asking you first." I pulled out the container of soup and held it in front of me. "I heard Julia hasn't been feeling well, and I couldn't sleep last night, so I made her some soup."

"Hey, Bernadette," Julia called from inside the apartment. I tried to rubberneck my way around Grady, but he took up the entire doorframe so I couldn't see around.

"Hey, honey!" I tried to yell through him. "I'm just dropping off some soup, but your bodyguard isn't letting me in."

"Who told you Julia wasn't feeling well?" Grady seemed awfully protective.

"Now you've got me worried." I looked up, trying to assess the look on his face. "Is she okay?" I handed him the soup.

"I think it's the flu. She went to the doctor, and they did a test. It should be back tomorrow." He softened his stance a little, and I could get a small peek around him.

Julia was sitting on their couch with a big blanket around her. She waved.

"Thank you!" she called out. "I'll let you know what the doctor says."

"You take care of yourself. Let me know if you need me to take off work and take care of you." I nodded. Then Grady stepped back into blocking my vision.

"I can take care of her. She'll be fine," Grady assured me.

"I was just offering my services," I assured him. "Not like I wouldn't do it for you."

"I've got her all taken care of." He took the soup. "Thank you for making this. We will have it tonight."

"Well, if you need me, I can be right here." I reached out and hugged my little boy, who was much bigger than I was now.

"Why aren't you sleeping?" he asked, shifting the conversation to me. "Are you okay?"

"I'm fine." I gnawed on the inside of my cheek, wondering if I should tell him about Mac.

"You look like you're champing at the bit to tell me something." Grady gave me a sideways look as though he was not trying to read me.

"Mac and I went on a date," I blurted out.

"I'm so glad you told him! I've been dying!" Julia exclaimed. She must have been listening to our conversation. "Mac has been in the best mood."

"Wait." Grady gave a slight shake of the head, like he was trying to get all the words in his head in order. "You knew my mom and Uncle Mac went on a date?"

"Technically, he's not your uncle." I made it clear.

"He's always acted like one, and you and Dad always told me to call him Uncle Mac." Grady made a good point, but he was also making it very clear he was concerned.

"If you don't approve, then it's not a big deal to not do it again." I gulped, thinking I was about to do it again tonight. In a few short hours.

"No. You're single. A grown woman. I guess…" He hesitated.

"Shut up, Grady! They are good together." Julia continued to put in her two cents from the couch. "Besides, don't you want your mom to have companionship with someone you love?"

There was that word again… companionship. Did people think I was too old for a real relationship? At what point did a relationship turn into companionship?

"It's fine." Grady bent down and kissed my cheek. "I'll call you tomorrow about Julia."

"Bye!" Julia waved me off before Grady shut the door.

I stood there with my nose nearly pressed up against the door for a few seconds before looking down at Buster.

"That was odd," I told him. I headed back down to the diner to find Mom and Dad waiting for me at the counter.

"That was a short visit." Mom was putting to-go containers in a bag.

"Yeah. Almost a little too short," I muttered before giving my dad a hug. "You doin' all right?"

"Honey, don't you worry about your old dad." He winked and patted my hand. "I'm worried about you finding another body."

"I'm good. I feel bad for Buster. I guess I've got to find him a good home." I looked down at the pup, and he was lying next to my feet. "I'm sure he's exhausted from running around all night and then being at the vet all day."

"Looks to me you found him a home." Dad smiled up at me from the stool.

"You?" My tone jumped up an octave.

"I think he looks comfortable with you." Dad winked, sending me into a tailspin with his observation. He knew how I stood on leaving a dog at home all day because of my job.

"I put some chocolate crinkles in there for you." Mom scrunched up her nose. "I made a fresh batch for the supper crowd."

"Can you put a few extra in? I'm having Mac over for supper, and I'm not sharing mine." I tried to soften the blow about me having Mac over by joking about me hoarding the cookies.

Mom threw her hands up to her mouth. Dad smacked the counter with his hand. Buster jumped to his feet.

"Hot dog! It's true." Dad yelled. "It's about dang time the two of you noticed the spark."

"Spark? Whoa." I put out a hand. "We are good friends."

"But you've never had Mac over for supper without someone else being there. Unless you've been keeping a secret?" Mom asked. "Luke Macum came in here today ordering some food for Lee's repass. He mentioned he saw you and Mac a little chummy over dinner at Pasanoe."

And why did I think I'd be saved from gossip? I should've known better.

"I wondered why you didn't tell me you were going out on a date, but I figured you'd tell us in your own time." Mom had a permanent smile on her face. I swear it was stuck there.

"You better get home." Dad was trying to rush me off. "Brush your hair too."

"Really?" I looked at him.

"Let me get those extra cookies." Mom took off like a jet to the kitchen.

"I'm not saying you're not beautiful. You are in your dad's eyes." My dad was backtracking.

"I get it, Dad." I bent down and kissed the top of his head. "I'll see y'all tomorrow with your mail."

"And all the details of your big date." Mom was filled with giddiness as she handed me the to-go bags. "I put some beans and cornbread in there so you didn't have to cook. The way to a man's heart is through his stomach, and I know he loves my beans."

"Thanks, Mom. Come on, Buster." I patted my leg, and like a good boy, he followed right alongside me.

Chapter 9

Buster and I made it back to the post office. I dropped off my mail carrier bag, and he and I got into the car to go home. The entire way, he seemed fine, even without some sort of car cage or seat belt. He sat straight up like a human in the passenger seat and even stared out the front window.

"It looks like you've been in a car before." I couldn't help praising the pup. My heart still ached for him, and I couldn't imagine what he'd gone through or the confusion he was feeling, but he seemed okay.

When we got to the farmhouse, the lights I left on for Rowena were all lit up, and the glow of the television peered through the family room window.

"Now, I've got a cat," I warned Buster. He looked at me and tilted his head. "Her name is Rowena, and I'm not sure how she's going to take you staying with me until we find you a home."

He tilted his head the other way as if he were really listening. Then he did the strangest thing. He lifted his right front leg and stretched it out, putting it on my hand like he was telling me it would all be okay.

"Fine then." I took a deep breath through my nose. "We will see how this all goes."

I reached into the back seat, grabbed the to-go bag Mom had prepared for us from the Wallflower, and got out of the car. Buster had moved over to the driver's seat and jumped out of the car behind me.

"Here we go." I wasn't sure what I would walk into. Rowena always greeted me at the door, and I figured tonight would be no different.

I put the key into the kitchen door's lock and turned it, praying and hoping we wouldn't scare poor Rowena into a heart attack. The orange tabby was used to being the queen of the house, and I'd never made her feel any differently.

"Good evening, Rowena. Did you have a good day?" I asked like I always did, pretending as if there weren't a big four-legged lab dog next to me, one that was at least seven times as big as she was.

Rowena didn't pay a bit of attention to me. The hair on her back stood straight up. She hissed a couple of times and bounced on top of the kitchen table. Just then, her automatic feeder went off, signaling it was six-thirty.

Buster ran over to the bowl to see what the fuss was all about.

"No, that's not yours," I told him and put the bag on the kitchen counter. "That's Rowena's." I looked at the time to make sure it was right. And it was. "Mac will be here any minute, but I need to feed you too."

Lights coming down the driveway shined right into the widows.

"Crap." I knew it was Mac. Of course it was. He was always on time. A great characteristic I admired about him since Richard was always late, but today I was hoping Mac would be a little late himself. "So much for trying to get myself all cleaned up."

Instead of fighting with myself, I took the food out that Mom had sent for Buster and Rowena.

Before I could even get the plates out of the cupboard, Mac was at the door. I waved him on in.

"Wow, Buster is here." He waved the bouquet of flowers at the dog. "Sorry." He laughed. "These are for you."

When he walked toward me, there was an uncomfortable air between us. It was like both of us were trying to figure out whether we should hug, kiss, or just laugh.

I picked kissing him on the cheek, but he must've also picked a kiss because he turned his head at the right moment and our lips touched. And touched some more and then a little deeper.

"I… ummm…" He pulled back, searching my eyes. "I would like to say I'm sorry, but I'm not."

"It's fine." I smiled and brushed the free hand over my hair. "I'm a mess." I hurried around him and laid the flowers on the table next to the food.

Rowena was still on high alert, with her hair still standing straight up and her eyes fixed on Buster. Buster was too busy trying to get Mac's attention.

"You aren't a mess." Mac glanced over at me with a softness in his eyes. "Let me get these in water while you feed them."

Mac busied himself looking for a vase under the sink and then filled it up. I got out the rice and chicken and sweet potato pieces Mom had sent for the fur babies. I divided the food between two plates while Mac arranged the flowers.

That was the thing with Mac. He knew his way around

my house like he lived here. I'd like to say it was because he and Richard were so close, but in truth, he knew his way around because he took Richard's place while Richard was away on business, which was at least half of each week.

"Say..." I had to banish the thoughts of that kiss from my head. I'd not kissed a man in... well, since I dated Richard. My lips were still tingling. "How much do I owe you for Buster's bill?"

"You can pay me with whatever it is in that bag your mom sent." He smiled, and I turned away. "Bernie, are you blushing?"

"Stop it." I couldn't do this anymore. "Really. What are we doing?"

"We are being adults who want companionship." That word rolled off his tongue.

"I'm sorry. I'm fifty years old, and I don't want companionship. That sounds like my parents." I put Buster's plate of food on the floor, setting the dish on the opposite side of the kitchen where Rowena's food was located. "I'm young. I want a real relationship."

"Is that right?" He walked up to me and tucked a strand of hair behind my ear. Then he slyly curled a hand behind my back, pulling me closer. "Relationship?"

His breath was hot on my face. My heart was beating so fast. I could see my own chest rising high and then falling. I knew he could feel it.

"Yeah," I whispered, feeling so secure in his arms. "A relationship."

He turned his head and bent it down ever so slightly as the phone in my pocket buzzed and rang, making us jump apart.

"It could be Grady about Julia. She's got the flu." I reached in my pocket and saw it was Angela Hafley. I'd been so lucky to get her phone number on a murder case not so long ago. "It's the sheriff." I looked at Mac.

"She's arresting us for wanting a relationship at our age," he joked.

I rolled my eyes and smiled.

"Hey, Angie. What's up?" I figured it was about Buster. "I'm sorry I forgot to call you about Buster."

"That's not why I'm calling, Bernadette." She sounded very official. "I have some bad news."

"Is everyone in my family okay?" I asked, my heart sinking into my toes. I eased down in the closest kitchen table chair.

"Your family is fine, I guess. I'm calling to let you know Lee Macum was murdered." Her words couldn't've shocked me more.

"Murdered?" I questioned and slid my gaze over to Mac, who was now sitting in the chair next to me. I moved the phone away from my mouth and whispered to Mac, "Lee was murdered."

His jaw dropped.

"Yes. Unfortunately, I'm going to have to ask you to come by the station in the morning, and I'm going to need full details of the events leading up to and when you found Lee." It was an order.

"Yeah, sure. Do you have a specific time?" I asked. I was going through my stops in my head and wondering how I could fit going to the station into my schedule.

"Can you stop by around lunch?" she asked.

"Yeah, sure," I agreed, knowing it would be a great time, since that would be right after my second loop, which included the downtown area and Little Creek Road. "I'll see you then."

I hung up the phone and put it on the table.

"Wow. I really didn't see anything to make me think he

was murdered." I was processing the images of how I'd found Lee on the floor. Mac put his hand on mine. "The door was open. I didn't even question it. And I'm sure Buster didn't jump up and open it himself." I was starting to rattle off all my memories of the scene. "Lee's eyes were open, and he had his hand in this really odd space." I glanced up at Mac. There was a questioning look on his face. "He has boxes all over the place. There is a tiny path in his house where you can walk. Literally, all boxes piled up." I snapped. "I recalled the weird open space and wondered how the boxes on top of it hadn't tumbled. Like that Jenga game." I nodded my head. Mac still had that expression on his face. "His hand was lying in that space with the stamp I'd given him from my dad the day before."

"Bernie," Mac said softly.

"Yeah." I continued to ramble, not letting him speak. "I asked him if he was moving, and he said heck no, over his dead body. Then I saw Luke at the nursing home inquiring about how he could get them in. There was the fight between Lee and Carla. And between Lee and Walter about your house." I gasped. "Do you think one of them killed him?"

Mac moved his hand from mine and pushed off the table to stand.

"I'm sorry. You're hungry." I shook off my sudden onset of sleuthing.

"I'm leaving." He stood over me.

"What? I thought we were having supper." I let out a nervous laugh.

"Me and you." He gestured between us. "Not me, you, Lee, Walter, Luke and Carla."

"Huh?" My brows furrowed, and I stood up.

"Bernie, I'm not sure if I can sit around and watch you try to figure out who killed Lee. You almost got killed trying to help me out, and I'm not sure I can go through that again." He walked toward the door and put his hand on the knob. "Good to see those two are getting along." He pointed at Buster and Rowena. They were both happily eating out of their own bowls. Rowena's fur had lain back down.

Mac walked out and shut the door behind him.

For the longest time after Mac left, I eased back down in the chair and watched the two fur babies as they did some sort of dance around each other. Buster switched between easing up to her and cowering down while she took some time walking around and taking a few sniffs of him.

It wasn't until Rowena touched her nose to Buster's that I finally took a breath.

"I guess our houseguest can stay a few days." I dragged the to-go bag over to me and thought about what had just happened between Mac and me.

I dug out one of the bowls of beans and the cornbread wrapped up in tinfoil. Instead of feeling sorry for myself and analyzing what happened, I stuffed my belly with not only my bowl of beans and serving of cornbread but also Mac's.

There was no sense in staying up late. When I headed back to bed after taking Buster outside, Rowena followed me back to the bedroom as normal and Buster followed us as if he knew what we were doing. I'd grabbed Buster's papers Kayla had given me from the vet clinic. All three of us climbed up in bed. Rowena made herself comfortable on her usual spot, Richard's pillow. And I watched as Buster found his spot next to me. His little face sat between his front paws, staring at me.

He finally drifted off to sleep in the same position while I read all about him. I was happy to see the great care Lee took of him, but why did Lee make me the emergency contact? It didn't make sense.

"Well, it does say you need to lose some weight, and they've cut back on your food." I looked down at the sleeping pup. I rubbed my hand over his neck, but he didn't budge. He'd had a long day. And night. "You know what helped me lose the extra pounds I put on after I lost Richard?" I didn't know whether I was telling Buster this for him or for me to come with grips about what I was about to say. "Walking my mail route. And I'm thinking you just might be able to go on the route with me now that I can't leave you here all day by yourself."

Buster's eyes never opened, but he did roll from lying on his stomach to turning onto his side, looking very comfortable in his new home.

Chapter 10

Chocolate Crunchie was the breakfast of choice for me. I'd already fed Rowena and Buster. I was happy they both remembered each other when we got up.

"Good morning, Iris." I answered my phone as I poured some coffee into my thermos. "You're up awfully early." I nestled the phone between my ear and shoulder and started to get my things together so I could go to work.

"I can't believe it. Lee was murdered. You did it again." She sounded more excited than sad about it.

"Huh?" I asked and watched as Rowena continued to get more sniffs of Buster. He was busy following me around the farmhouse.

"You found another dead body. You've become known as more than a mail carrier." She laughed.

"What on earth are you talking about?" I asked her.

"Lucy Drake's show this morning. She told the world how you found Lee, and now it's an active homicide. Get this"—she paused, building up to a big climax—"she's calling you the mail carrier who is delivering more than the

TONYA KAPPES

mail. She's delivering bodies to the morgue. A mail carrier magnet for murder."

"What?" My jaw dropped. "Magnet for murder?"

"Mail carrier magnet for murder." Iris laughed. "I about peed myself when I heard it come through my car radio."

I sat there stunned for a second.

"I'm going to stop in and see her this morning." I made a mental note not to just deliver the mail to WSCG radio station but to actually make an appearance to Lucy Drake, the morning DJ.

"It's all in good fun when we are having yet another crisis." Iris was probably right, but I didn't embrace the new nickname. "How's Buster? Rowena like him?"

"They are actually getting along pretty well, and I've made a decision to keep him, but I have one small problem," I told her. "I'm not sure what to do with him during the day."

"Easy." Iris always saw things as easy and always had a solution. I braced myself to hear what she had in mind. "Take him with you. Clip a leash and go."

"Actually, that's not a bad idea." I didn't tell her that I'd already considered it, but it's always to get good confirmation.

One, walking would help his weight issue. And two, he wouldn't be here all day with no one to let him out.

"And you can sic him on Lucy Drake." Iris giggled so loudly I had to remove the phone from my ear. "Listen, I've got to go. I'm dropping off donuts to the beautification committee for their last meeting before the big day."

"Watch how Carla reacts for me." I still had my little mental list of suspects, and I was definitely going to tell Angie all about them when I went there today.

"Carla? Why?" Iris asked.

"She seems like a likely suspect to me. Don't you think?" I pondered whether I might be wrong.

"I never even thought of it," Iris said with a gasp. "Do you think? I mean, she's been so vocal about her distaste for him since she entered Sugar Creek Gap into the contest."

"I wasn't going to say anything, but she did ask my mom to put arsenic in the biscuits Mom gave me to deliver to him when I dropped off his mail." Chills ran up my body. I shuddered thinking about it.

"Oh no." Iris cried out, "I just can't believe this world. And to think Lee's death might be over some silly messy yard."

"Don't be going around saying it's her because that's just my theory. Do you think it's dumb?" I asked.

"Dumb? What?"

"I wasn't even going to mention it, but Mac came over last night for supper. We kissed." I waited for Iris to scream.

Her scream lasted about three seconds, followed by a few "oh my Gods."

"But then he told me he couldn't continue if I was going to stick my nose in Lee's murder because he couldn't stand it if I got hurt, and he left." I gave an abbreviated version in which I left out how Angie had called and interrupted what was looking to be another kiss.

"How dare he," she said. "You have a knack for this sort of thing, and I'm going to help out. I've got to go, but I'll keep my eyes and ears on Carla."

"You let me know." I hung up the phone and slipped it into the pocket of my work pants before I grabbed the thinner zip-up work coat.

Even though the season was turning to spring, the mornings still held a bit of coldness in the air to go along with the chills I already felt from thinking Carla killed Lee, so I had to bundle up.

"Rowena, you be a good girl." I patted my leg and grabbed my keys. "Let's go, Buster. You get to be my co-worker."

I wasn't sure how my boss would take this change, but when I got to the post office, it was already buzzing with mail carriers, and all of them loved on Buster. Of course, all their questions about how I found Lee made me a little late for the nursing home.

"Oh, Bernadette," Vivian said in a voice oozing with southern sorrow. "I'm so sad to hear of Lee's death. I knew you two were close."

The smell of bacon and waffles came from the dining room and made my stomach growl.

"Ummm." I swallowed, trying to wet my dry mouth. "Why do you think we were close?"

This was a recurring observation from everyone I'd come into contact with today. Even my co-workers at the post office said this about Lee and me.

"Buster, for one." Vivian bent down and patted him. "And the fact Lee welcomed you into his home." She stood up, shaking her head. Her eyes filled with sadness. "To think someone killed him."

"About that." I knew this was a perfect time to ask her about her chat with Luke. "You know I was in here when Iris was calling bingo, and I couldn't help but overhear Luke Macum say something about losing his memory."

Vivian stood up a little taller. Her face became stern as she tugged her chin in the air and looked down past her nose at me. A couple of residents walked by.

"Bernie!" Vince Caldwell, one of my favorite residents,

waved to me on his way to the dining room. "Come see me."

I waved back.

"Are you asking me to break my confidentiality I pride myself on to tell you the private conversation between Luke Macum and me?" she asked loudly, as if I'd stolen her own apple pie recipe and learned of a secret ingredient. We all keep those sorts of little tidbits to ourselves. "Do you think Luke killed his uncle?" She crossed her arms, taking a sudden interest. "I mean"—she leaned in a little bit—"I can probably tell you but not in front of the residents." She slid her gaze to Vince and the other resident. "I can't have them thinking I tell their secrets. But I know you really helped on the last murder in Sugar Creek Gap, so I might have some information if it will bring Lee to eternal rest." She made the sign of the cross as if she'd turned into Sugar Creek Gap's own Mother Theresa.

It took every fiber of my being not to roll my eyes at her.

She motioned for me to follow her into her office, which was located right there in the lobby behind that big glass window. She took a seat behind the big wooden desk while Buster lay on the floor and I sat in the chair.

"According to Luke, Lee has been saving everything. Even every little piece of mail you gave him." Her eyes grew. "In fact, he was eating Buster's food."

"What?" My face contorted. I just couldn't believe it.

"Mmm-hmmm, that's what Luke told me." Her lips pinched with subtle nods of the head. "He said Lee has been forgetting to lock his doors at night too." Everything she was saying didn't at all go with the Lee Macum I knew. "These are all signs of dementia, and Luke feared Lee was too far gone to live alone."

"I don't know, Vivian." I sat back in the chair and

pondered what she was saying. "I saw Lee every day but Sunday, and he seemed sharp as a tack to me."

"I'm just telling you what I know." She made a pish-posh noise. "It don't matter now, because he's not coming here."

"Did you have a spot open for him?" I asked, knowing there had been a long wait list.

"We only had one of the single-bedroom assisted-living rooms open, which is the costliest because of it being one bedroom when all the open living rooms are full. But Luke didn't seem to care to pay for the ten-thousand-a-month bill because he said Lee had an extensive stamp collection that was worth a ton, and he was sure he was guardian of Lee's estate." She drummed her fingers on the desk. "Seeing he's Lee's only heir and all."

"Well, thanks." I stood up, and Buster took my lead. "I've got to get this mail delivered, or you're going to have an uprising," I teased and hoisted the bag on my shoulder.

"I'm sorry I couldn't be any more help. It's a terrible situation, and I hope they find his killer fast." She sighed. "Poor Luke."

"Yeah, poor Luke," I muttered to Buster on my way out of her office. "Poor Luke, nothing."

I hurried myself down to the community mailboxes and quickly got those filled. Then I headed over to the apartments on the nursing home property where my parents lived.

It was owned by the nursing home, but the apartments were single-living arrangements perfect for elderly couples who didn't want to do yard work or even cook if they didn't feel like it. They were able to use all the amenities the nursing home had to offer, including an indoor pool, a workout room, a library, a couple different cafes, and the dining hall, not to mention the daily field trips and the fun activities the administration planned.

Mom and Dad loved it there, as did my good buddy Vince.

"You're late," Vince scolded when he saw me coming back down the hall to go out the front door.

"I was just heading to your place." I smiled at him. "Want to walk with me?"

"Yes, but I brought this little feller something." He pulled a piece of bacon from a paper towel in his hand. "I'm sure you don't approve, but a little bit won't hurt."

I kept my mouth shut and got a little concerned Buster might get a belly ache, since I didn't know him well. He gobbled up the bacon.

"New employee?" Vince asked on our way out the door. "Or are you scared someone is going to kill you on the route?"

"So you heard." We crossed the street from the main building to the apartments and down the sidewalk while I told him about Lee.

"Any suspects?" he asked with a gleam in his eye and stared at me under his bushy grey brows.

Vince was retired from the FBI for fifteen years now. When he left the Bureau, he wanted a small, quiet little town with a good view, and Sugar Creek Gap was that for him. And he even had some access to various websites and codes that'd helped us in the last murder investigation. He was very knowledgeable.

"Well, it's no secret how Carla has been running around town talking bad about Lee and his house. Then there's his nephew Luke, who I was told was going to place him in the nursing home. I can't forget the fight I heard between Lee and Walter Ward about the property or the fight Lee had with Carla. All three could be suspects, but I'm not sure. None of them seem like killers." I handed him his mail and grabbed the mail for the next stops out of my bag.

I could tell he was noodling over what I was saying, processing it like I'd seen him do the last time.

"I've got to go to the station at lunch and give the sheriff my statement," I told him. "I'll run all my thoughts by her and let you know what she says."

"Sounds good." He shook his mail at me. "I'll do some background checks on your suspects and let you know what I find out."

"Perfect." I smiled. "I'll see you tomorrow. Or later if you call with some information."

While Buster and I delivered the mail to the rest of the apartment residents, I didn't give any more thought to Vince and the pride he took in trying to help out. No matter how much Carla, Walter, and Luke could be suspects, I really couldn't figure out exactly why each one of them would honestly have the guts to kill someone, much less Lee. Maybe Mac was right. It wasn't my job to solve murders, much less point fingers, when the law stated that everyone was innocent until proven guilty.

Buster and I stopped by the post office on our way back from the nursing home to Main Street, where my second loop would be delivered. I grabbed the mail already sorted for me, and we started across the street at Sugar Creek Gap Veterinarian Clinic. I had a box of syringes the staff needed to sign for, and as quickly as I could get that out of my hands, the better.

Buster trotted right on in when I opened the door. I caught Kayla's eyes. She was taking payment from a customer. Buster and I waited patiently. His tail was swishing to the right and left, dusting the floor. He was itching to look in the carrier sitting on the floor next to the customer.

When he looked up at me, I told him, "Be a good boy." I wasn't sure how many commands Buster knew. I only knew he was really good.

The customer picked up the carrier and smiled at me when she noticed Buster wasn't budging.

"He's a good boy." The customer looked down and smiled at Buster.

"He sure is. And he's looking for a new home," Kayla chimed in, though she didn't need to.

"I'm sorry, he's not. He's mine." I glared at Kayla. I knew she was passionate about animals, and so was I, but she didn't have to be flat-out mean. "Kayla is mistaken."

I wasn't going to take that from her, and I'd definitely address it with Doc Olson when I saw her.

"I thought you said..." Kayla started to overstep once again.

"I do have the right to change my mind." I gave her the sweet southern bless-your-heart smile to avoid giving her a good cussing out. "Is Doc Olson available?"

"I can sign for whatever." Kayla was used to getting the packages, but I really wanted to see Doc. She put her hands out.

"That's okay. I'd like Doc Olson to sign if you don't mind." I didn't move or change my mind.

"Fine. You'll have to wait. She's with a client." Kayla went back to doing some paperwork. Buster and I sat down. "Mail carrier magnet for murder," I heard her mumble.

"What did you say?" I jumped up, and Buster followed.

The door to the waiting area opened. Doc Olson and a woman with a small pet carrier walked out.

"Is everything okay?" Doc Olson asked me and looked at Kayla.

"Can I see you?" I asked her interrupting Kayla as she stumbled over her words.

The customer walked up to Kayla to pay her bill, taking Kayla's attention.

"Absolutely. Do we need a patient room?" She pointed at Buster. "Or office?"

"Office." That was my way of telling her that it wasn't about Buster. "And if you don't mind signing for this one." I held the package out, and when she took it, I plucked the pen from my jacket pocket.

"Thank you." She scribbled on the piece of paper that I'd take back to the post office to let the syringe company know she received it. She motioned for me to follow her through the door. "I don't mind if Kayla signs for those."

"I know, but I wanted to talk to you, so I just waited. Kayla was busy with a customer." I really wanted to complain about Kayla, but I figured it would be best to keep my mouth shut.

Doc Olson's office was pretty basic. Her desk that had nothing on it. Her diplomas were framed and hanging on the wall. There was a coat rack with her purse dangling from one of the arms. Simple.

"Buster is a good dog. I hope you find a home for him soon." She eased down into one of the chairs in front of her desk, signaling me to sit in the one next to her.

"I'm keeping him." I told her and sat down as she suggested. We both gave him some good rubs when he walked between us.

"Oh, Kayla said you didn't know you were the emergency contact." She looked confused.

"I didn't, but I still want to keep him. He and Rowena

get along. But that's not why I'm here." So much for taking my own advice. I just couldn't help myself. "Last night you mentioned you needed to go to the beautification committee because you've seen an uptick in poisoned clients."

"Yes. I had to go complain about Carla spraying it all over the place." She shook her head. "Carla was so mad. She said people needed to keep their animals in their own yards, not the places she was spraying." She snorted. "I told her the places she was spraying are public and pet owners have the right to walk their dogs, cats, or even lizards if they want to."

"Not that it's any of my business, but I feel like I owe it to Lee and Buster to help figure out who might've killed Lee." I was hoping she understood that I was talking about Carla being on my suspect list.

"He was killed? As in murdered?" Dr. Olson hadn't heard.

"Oh yeah. No thanks to Lucy Drake, my new title is mail carrier magnet for murder." I rolled my eyes. "Or something silly like that."

"That's ridiculous. Anyway, how was he killed?" Her brows furrowed.

"Poisoned." That one word made it appear that her thoughts had frozen. "Poisoned," she gasped and looked away.

"Yes. But I'm not sure what kind, which is why I'm here. Do you know what kind of poison you're finding in your clients?" Just then, I looked down at Buster, and I did owe it to him and Lee to help out as much as I could.

As much as I wanted to see how things progressed with Mac and me, I wasn't going to change who I was just to please him. I'd already been there and done that with

Richard. Sometimes I got mad at Richard because he didn't realize how much his big secret killed me or how much I'd changed over our marriage to make sure he was living his best life, which meant putting mine on the back burner. Even though I was pretty sure Mac didn't have a second relationship, I was sure I wouldn't go back to the person I was when I was married to Richard.

"It wasn't like I did the chemical panels to figure it out. And the animals obviously can't tell me what they are feeling, so I have to go on diagnosis by their symptoms. They all have common symptoms." She stood up and walked around the desk, where she opened one of the desk drawers and took out a notebook. She flipped through it and began reading. "Vomiting, diarrhea, lethargic, stopped eating. . ."

She rattled off words I didn't even understand.

Finally, she looked up. "All poison that is tied to common household products like weed killer." She scratched her neck. "Do you think Carla killed Lee? I mean, she was going full force last night at the meeting, saying how she didn't want to speak ill of the dead but wanted to know who was going to go ask Luke when he would clean up the joint. Then she offered to pay out of her own pocket for someone to come if Luke didn't budge."

"Did anyone agree?" I asked.

"I wasn't around for the end of the conversation, but I did see Lucy Drake there." Her shoulders dropped. "What poison did Lee die of?"

"Oh, I don't know." I shook my head. "All I know was that he was poisoned."

"Could it have been his own doing?" Her words made me pause. "I mean, I heard he was hoarding and had touches of dementia."

"Who told you that?" I asked.

"Not that I like to gossip, but I do think this needs to be explored. Maybe I should call Sheriff Hafley." She gnawed on her lip.

"Actually, I have a meeting with her at noon, so I'm more than happy to tell her what you want her to know." I did make it sound like I was going to help Angie, but I didn't say I was, so I let Doc Olson believe what she wanted to believe. Especially if it made her talk.

And it did.

"Well, Vivian from the nursing home told me. She said Luke was going to spend a lot of money to get Lee in the nursing home. When I told her I couldn't believe Luke could afford it because he's on a payment plan here with his last vet bill for his cat, she told me about Lee's stamp collection. Apparently he had a very expensive stamp that, if he sold it to the right person, would bring him a lot of money. Enough to cover Lee's nursing home expenses and then some." She sighed. "My own mother had dementia, so I understand how Lee could've poisoned himself. My mom was always picking up some sort of cleaner and sprinkling it in her coffee, thinking it was sugar."

Doc Olson rambled on about her mom, and I was very sorry for that, but Luke said Lee had a very expensive stamp, and it made me think of the letter Lee said he was waiting for. A letter he said he needed to sign for and was in his daily digest email from the USPS. I still hadn't received any such letter from Monica who did all the sorting and gave me those letters.

I had to ask Angie if she found any stamps in the house, and if she had seen any certified letter for Lee. What about her mention that Luke couldn't pay his bill in full and was on a payment plan?

"I sure hate to hear about Luke's cat. Did he have

surgery?" I asked to find out exactly how much of a bill he couldn't pay.

"His cat is a she, and she didn't have surgery. Just the usual checkup."

A knock at the door interrupted us.

Kayla's head popped out from behind the door.

"Your next client is here." She looked past me and at Doc Olson, and then Kayla left.

"I'm sorry to cut this short, but let me know if you need any more information or if the sheriff needs anything. I'm sorry I didn't test for a specific poison." She walked me to the door leading to the lobby. "I just know they are all having symptoms from common household products, and it can't be a coincidence with Carla spraying that dang weed killer all over."

She only said what I was thinking. The factual evidence was building against Carla. And I thought about that evidence as I quickly delivered the mail to the shops downtown. That she said to lace the biscuits with arsenic was reason enough for me to believe, plus the animals were getting sick from her weed killer, and Lee just so happened to die from poisoning. Apparently, she didn't have an ounce of sorrow for the poor man, according to Doc Olson, who mentioned that Carla asked how quickly they could get Lee's place cleaned up.

"We need to tell all that to Angie," I told Buster before I headed into Tranquility Wellness to drop off their mail. Buster sat next to the doors on the sidewalk when I went inside the shops to deliver their mail. He was so good. The company wasn't bad either.

The Wallflower was packed when I stopped in there. From the mumblings and murmurs I heard when I walked, I could tell they were talking about the mail carrier magnet for murder. A few of them even shuffled away from me.

"Seriously?" I handed Mom her mail.

"You know we are very superstitious around here." Even though my mom was joking, it was still apparent that nearly everyone in here believed it, because even the men who sat at the stools at the counter had moved down a couple of stools.

"Funny," I told them and glared. One of those men was my dad.

"It's all in good humor." Dad scooted back down and patted Buster on the head. "Peg, can you get Buster a drink?"

"Hhmmm." My mom headed back to the kitchen.

"Any new gossip I don't know about?" I asked my dad and looked around, knowing they'd been hearing all sorts of things. "The same regular thing about Carla losing her mind about the contest."

The bell over the diner door dinged. The hush that fell over the joint made me look to see what silenced everyone.

Luke Macum and Walter Ward had walked through the door and taken a seat at the corner two-topper on the far left side.

Mom rushed over, shooing the waitress away.

"That's where you get it from." My dad didn't bother hiding his pointing finger.

"What?" I pretended like I didn't know and went behind the counter to get Buster's water bowl from Mom, which I practically threw down when she came back from the kitchen.

Dad simply touched his nose.

"Both you girls are nosy." He shook his head and picked up his cup of coffee.

"You wouldn't want us any other way." I kissed him on the top of his head and bent down to give Buster his water.

"Why don't you leave him here, and I'll drive him out

to the farmhouse later today?" Dad really liked dogs. He always had. "I ain't got nothing better to do."

"Are you sure?" Not that I wanted to get rid of Buster, but I wasn't sure what I was going to do with him when I went to the sheriff's to see Angie.

It was all new to Buster and me. He seemed to be doing a lot better than I was. I was worried someone would take him or he'd wander off. It was all part of the learning process— each of us was learning about the other.

"I'm positive. I need to get to know him, don't I?" Dad smiled.

"How did you know I was going to keep him?" I asked, leaning my hip against the counter.

"I could see it in your eyes when you walked in right through that door." My dad and I had a different sort of bond than the one I had with my mom. Mom taught me life lessons in the form of baking. My dad, he taught me life lessons on the farm and during hunting season, which I hated.

In fact, I never killed a thing with a beating heart in my life. Not even a gnat. But it was the long hours we spent in a deer stand or crouched down behind a tree trunk or even fishing in one of the many small ponds around Sugar Creek Gap that gave Dad and me the time to talk and ponder.

"Thanks, I think he wants to stay." I pointed down at Buster. He was lying under Dad's feet fast asleep. "I think the walking has already tuckered him out." I shook a parental finger at Dad. "Don't feed him."

"Don't feed him?" Mom had walked up and acted as if I'd committed a carnal sin.

"Don't. Doc Olson said he needs to lose weight. And if he's not walking the rest of the way, then he doesn't need to eat until he gets home." I pushed myself off the counter. "What are those two discussing?"

"Luke and the ambulance chaser?" Mom glanced back over at them. "What do you think? When Luke is going to let him sell the house."

"Did you hear anything?" I asked.

"Are you snooping around again?" Mom replied. "Because if you are, I have to tell you that Luke was in here last night waiting for some stamp collector to meet him. From out of town." Mom made it seem so dark and sinister. "The collector never showed, but that's not the worst part." She leaned to me and whispered in my ear. "Luke's bank card." She pulled back, her brows rising quickly . "Declined. I had to give him the meal."

Oh Lord.

I glanced at Luke and Walter on my way out the door. It was time to meet Angie. How was I going to tell her Luke was also one of my suspects? She seemed very fond of him on the phone, which made me think he was one step ahead of the investigation and had very cleverly aligned himself with Angie to get the scoop and cover his tracks. I just couldn't help but think if he had money problems, wouldn't he try to get the stamp, and Lee didn't want to give it to him. Maybe he poisoned his own uncle.

I couldn't wait to tell Angie all my ideas so this could be wrapped up fast.

Little Creek Road delivery would have to wait until after lunch. I'd gotten stopped a few times about the murder, which really put me behind. Of course I already knew it would, but I liked to keep my ears open for little tidbits that might be clues.

You never know what you'll get from gossip. The truth had to be weeded out.

The sheriff's department was across the street from the

Wallflower, and I knew I couldn't stop myself from going into the WSCG radio station building unless I crossed Main Street in front of the diner. I would definitely see Lucy Drake on my way to deliver the mail on Little Creek Road.

Angie was waiting for me and tapping her foot when I stepped into the door. She pointed at her watch.

"Do you want to know how many people stopped me today about this murder while I was delivering their mail?" I asked her.

"Fine. I don't have all day," she said over her shoulder as she practically ran, motioning me to follow her. "I'm going to have to record your statement because I don't have any extra hands to type it out."

She opened the door to one of their interview rooms, which sometimes served as the snack room for the staff. Angie pointed for me to sit down and then grabbed the paper plates and napkins from the center of the table, replacing them with a tape recorder.

She leaned over and pushed the record button.

"I'm Bernadette Butler, USPS mail carrier," I started but, Angie met me with a sly eye. "What?" I asked her. She slightly shook her head. "I remember all this from last time," I added.

"We can skip the particulars. I want you to start with where you were taking Buster back to his home." She waved for me to go on.

"I thought it was odd that the gate latch was unhooked, only because I know Lee never left it open because of Buster. He loved Buster so much." I actually missed the feller. "He is so good. He slept in the bed with me..."

"Bernie." Angie shut me up. "Stick with what happened."

"Yeah. Right." I sucked in a deep breath. It was so easy

for me to get off track, but I knew it would make Angie madder if I tried to say anything other than the facts, so stating the facts was what I did. I told her that I found it weird the door to the house was open because it took Lee a long time to unlock the doors when I delivered the mail and that I could always hear him locking them back when I left. "Which brings me to why I think Carla killed him. You said it was poison. Well, she said to me in the diner before Lee was killed to put arsenic in the biscuits my mom sent with me to give to him."

"Whoa!" Angie stood up from the chair across from me and put her hand up. She leaned over the table and clicked off the tape recorder. "I didn't ask you to give me your opinion on who you think killed Lee. I asked you to tell me the exact details of how you found him and up until I got there."

"But you have to hear who I think did it." I couldn't believe she was stopping me. "I have good reason to believe…"

"That Carla did it… yada, yada." It was like Angie's head was shaking constantly because she'd been shaking it ever since I walked in. "You stick with delivering the mail. I'll stick with the investigation." She took a couple of steps back and opened the door. "I'll let you know if I need anything else."

"You don't want to hear about Carla already poisoning the animals in Sugar Creek Gap? Because Doc Olson told me all about it." I continued to talk to her, though she faced away from me, as we walked down the hall and back to the door where I'd entered. "Or how Carla wants to win the make-our-city or whatever it is award so bad that she'd kill…"

"That I'd kill?" I heard Carla's voice.

I closed my eyes and turned slightly to where the voice

was coming from, hoping that when I opened them, I wouldn't see Carla standing there in the flesh.

No such luck.

"Bernie." Angie had already opened the door and pointed for me to go.

"Don't forget to light up your cart tomorrow." Carla had to get in the last word before Angie shut the door.

Chapter 11

That was not exactly how I thought that would go. I admit I overstepped my boundaries at times, but I had some really good information on my hands, though it appeared Angie had some knowledge of Carla because Carla wouldn't be there if Angie hadn't called her in.

"Don't forget to light up your cart," I said in mockery of Carla when I got to the bridge on Short Street, where my duck friend lived.

The bridge was a walking bridge that went over Little Creek and led to Little Creek Road. I had a duck friend who always greeted me at the top of the street and then again at the bottom. Since Little Creek was a dead-end road, I crossed over the walking bridge that put me between the vet clinic and Social Knitwork. The bridge was a perfect place to head back to the post office to get my third loop of mail.

I didn't spend much time with the duck because I was running so late that I knew the front porch ladies would be waiting very impatiently for me.

Boy, was I right. The four of them practically rushed

up the street to meet me when they saw me turn the corner from Short Street. The only thing I began to think about was Mac, and I pulled his mail out of my bag as I met the ladies in front of his house.

"Where have you been?" Harriette was the ringleader. "I could be a millionaire and not even know it."

"That's a good point." Gertrude threw her two cents in. "We really want to know if we got the invitations to the bridal shower because we heard June from our bridge club got her invitation, and she's never picked up a finger to help no one, much less poor Zeke."

Poor Zeke? First off, he was not poor, and that man had so many meals dropped off to him when I was delivering his mail that I knew he was far from lonely. Thinking of that made me wonder if I scared Mac off too soon, and then I'd be like these ladies, begging for an invitation to a bridal shower only to get closer to companionship at their age.

"Let me get Mac's mail up to him, and I'll be right over," I told them. "And to be honest, I didn't even look at the mail today."

"Oh honey, you had better things to do." Ruby shooed the woman back towards Harriette's house. "We have some homemade pimento cheese finger sandwiches today. You come on over and grab you a couple."

The front porch ladies took their sweet time getting over to Harriette's house, the entire time watching to see what was going to happen with me. The closer I got to the steps of Mac's front porch, the more my heart raced. I swear the sweat from my hands were making sweat stains on the mail I was holding.

A huge sigh of relief swept through me after I slipped the mail through the mail slot and didn't hear footsteps to come get it. I was very thankful he wasn't home.

"Hey." The voice made me jump around. Mac was in the side yard between his house and Harriette's house with a spay in his hand.

"You scared me to death." I held my hand to my heart.

"You were trying to get away without seeing me, weren't you?" He threw the spade on the ground and tugged off his gloves as he walked around the front porch and then jogged up the two steps.

The front porch ladies had taken their perch on Harriette's porch but were eerily silent.

"How did Buster do?" Mac asked.

"He did fine." I wasn't sure where my feelings stood. The sadness I felt earlier had been replaced by anger and now just plain confusion.

"How is Rowena with him?" he asked in a genuine tone.

"Fine, Mac." I grabbed the strap of my mail bag and moved past him to go down the steps so I could get on my way. "Great. Really great." I turned when I got to the sidewalk leading to his front gate. "Actually, we are *all* great."

I looked over at the front porch ladies. They all snapped their heads forward as if I didn't know they were watching Mac and me. They didn't have to tell me that they knew he'd come over and had soon come back home. They knew everything, and I wasn't sure how.

"Ladies." I pinched a smile, took my mail bag off, and put it on the ground. Then I started distributing their mail. "I don't see Wayne Brady," I told Harriette, "so I'm guessing you didn't win Publishers Clearing House, but good news." I waved her mail in the air.

"I got an invitation from Zeke?" Her eyes lit up.

"Nope." I held her mail out to her. "You got another chance from Publishers Clearing House."

"You make fun of me now, but when they do show up

with my big ten-foot million-dollar check, I'll be laughing all the way to the bank." She snatched the mail from me.

Millie Barnes was super-quiet.

"Are you feeling better?" I asked Millie. Her shoulders tensed. Her face hardened.

"I'm fine." She spoke in very short, precise words.

"I was worried about you passing out yesterday at Lee's house." I could tell she was definitely not fine. I really cared for these women, as if they were my aunts or other kinds of relatives. They'd been so kind and had become family to me over the past ten years, though I knew them before. It wasn't until I actually did their mail route that I got to know them.

"I said I'm fine." She squeezed her brows together. "Now drop it and eat a pimento cheese sandwich." She gestured for Harriette to pass the serving tray my way.

"And give me your mug so I can fill it up with some tea." Harriette had me dig through my mail bag for my empty thermos in exchange for the tray of finger sand-wiches. Then she took the thermos inside her house to fill it with her homemade sweet tea.

"Go on and tell her, Millie. It ain't like we don't know her night didn't go so well." Gertrude spewed my suspicions.

"You tell us first what happened with you and Mac," Mille responded slowly.

"I'm not sure Mac likes me for me or the person he knows as Richard's wife, Grady's mom." When I said this out loud, it really did hit home with me. "He doesn't like me snooping around in Lee's murder."

Millie gave an obvious hard swallow. Harriette broke the tension when she came back out to the porch and handed me my thermos.

"You're looking into Lee's murder?" Ruby asked,

easing up on the edge of the rocking chair and used her toe to keep it still from moving.

"I'm not sure if you knew that Lee had me as Buster's emergency contact." When I looked at Millie, she was picking at the sandwich in her hands as if she were trying to avoid me. "I had no idea until Doc Olson told me. I took Buster home with me, and he fit right in with Rowena and me."

I couldn't help but smile. Millie looked up with tears in her eyes.

"I even brought him to work with me, but you know my parents. They talked me into letting him hang out with them for a few hours." I shrugged and looked over towards Mac's house just to make sure he couldn't hear me, but it appeared as if he'd already gone inside. "I'm afraid Mac doesn't really embrace the need I have to help Angie find Lee's killer."

Millie perked up.

"Did he say that?" Harriette asked through a mouthful of finger sandwiches.

"He said that he couldn't take it if I got hurt, so he didn't agree with me snooping." Those might not have been his exact words, but it was his exact feelings about me nosing around. "Clearly, I don't see it as snooping."

"You're not!" Millie found her voice. "You're embracing your inner Jessica Fletcher. She was a writer. You're a mail carrier. You do it! You help figure out what happened to my Lee."

The silence fell over the group. Millie gulped. She eased back into the porch swing like a turtle going back into its shell.

"'My Lee'?" If she thought that slipped by me, she had another thing coming.

Then it smacked me in the face.

"Millie, you passed out because you were dating Lee and…." When I saw the sadness cross her face and her shoulders droop, I knew I hit the nail on the head. "I am so sorry. I had no idea."

"They only knew because they are nosy." She pointed to Gertrude, Ruby, and Harriette separately.

"We can't help it if we are old and can't sleep," Ruby shot back with a snarl.

"And if you didn't have the big flashlight leading the way down the sidewalk, I wouldn't've called the sheriff's office." Gertrude had called the sheriff.

I tried desperately not to laugh, but it fell out of my mouth, sending a ripple effect through the rest of the ladies, even Millie.

"Oh, you should've seen her. She thought she was something." Gertrude got up and pretended she was Millie with a flashlight in her hand, acting out the night they were talking about.

Even Millie chuckled.

"We were companions." Millie threw out that stupid word.

"Companionship doesn't extend into the night. We might be old and can't sleep, but we all fall asleep." Harriette looked at Millie and smiled. "But we were happy for her and Lee. He was a crochety old thing."

"He was very kind to me." Millie gave a slight smile. "And I'm not surprised you were Buster's emergency contact. Lee really thought a lot of you."

"That's so kind." I walked over and bent down in front of her, and then I put my hand on top of hers. "I'm sorry. I didn't know about your relationship, and if it bothers you that I'm looking into things, I'll stop."

"Heck no!" She jerked her hand out from underneath mine. "I told the gals here that we were all going to look into people, and now that I know you're on the case, I feel much better."

"Yeah. We were all talking about it this morning. That's why we've been waiting for you to get here." Ruby nodded. "We think you can help."

"I can." I knew Millie could be a great source of information. "But first I have to deliver the mail." I walked back over to my mail bag, which was empty but for Lee's mail, and strapped it back across my body. "Can I come over tonight after work?" I asked Millie. "Lord knows I don't have plans."

"That would be perfect," Millie said, and the gals all looked as though they agreed. "I'll fix something special for us to eat. We love to eat."

"If it's okay with you, I'll stop by the diner and grab something to eat. If you don't mind if Buster comes, that'd be great." I wanted to make sure, even though Millie was apparently around Buster more than I knew. Still, some people didn't like dogs. Who were they? I had no idea, but they didn't.

"Of course he can come. I welcome it." Millie rubbed her hands together. "Ladies, we are on the case."

The thought that Millie had gone in and out of Lee's house for no telling how long they'd been dating was going to be helpful for my case. I would be able to get an idea of what Lee really thought of Carla and Luke as well as his thoughts on my less likely suspect, Walter Ward.

Just out of curiosity, I did want to know how she felt about the hoarding situation. I'd been in Millie's house a few times over the past ten years. Really, I only went inside the door on especially cold winter days when she needed to sign for something, but the temperature had to be practically freezing for the front porch ladies not to be on their perches. Each one of them had invested in front porch heaters. It also helped that their gossip was so hot that it kept them from freezing.

Still, Millie's home was not at all hoarding. Her furniture was pretty outdated, but she was not collecting things like Lee did. I just wanted to pick her brain on what she thought of all that.

Instead of going down towards Lee's house, I knew his mail could wait, and there was nothing in there but junk anyway. Besides, yellow crime scene tape was wrapped around his entire front porch. I could only imagine the hissy fit Carla would throw over seeing it. That would surely knock us out of the Make Kentucky Colorful state campaign.

I headed back towards the top of the street to cross the bridge on Short Street. I knew my duck friend wouldn't be there because he was already at the other end of Little Creek waiting for me, but I had other plans.

My plans involved Lucy Drake.

I had a bone to pick with her, and I was going to pluck her clean.

WSCG was located on the corner of Short Street and Main Street, across from the courthouse and sheriff's department. I was switching up my route to go that way so I could head back to the post office and grab my third loop of mail, but Lucy Drake was on my radar.

The front of the radio station was one big window that showed the guts of the studio where all the station's programs took place. I generally loved walking by and waving at the DJ on air. Usually.

When I turned the corner to Main Street, I looked at Lucy Drake. Her back was to the window. She wore big earphones and did a little dance around the studio to whatever it was she was playing on the radio.

I smacked the glass with a flat palm, causing the glass

to reverberate so much it made her jump around with a startled look in her eyes. She shuffled backwards when she saw who I was. Her mouth fell open, and her fingers touched her parted lips.

"I've got a bone to pick with you." I mouthed and pointed a finger.

Touching her throat, she turned away and took her earphones off. Then she took the first steps toward her door, and I hoped she was coming outside to see me.

I waited patiently. I really did. For about five minutes.

"Bernie!" Sheriff Angie called from across the street. "What are you doing?"

"Sheriff! She's harassing me!" Lucy Drake had whipped open the door.

"Harassing you?" I couldn't believe Lucy Drake had called the sheriff's department on me. "I think it's the other way around, Lucy. You're calling me names on the radio. That's harassment."

I stalked over to the glass front door of the radio station. Lucy slammed it in my face and locked it.

"Bernie, this isn't going to solve anything." Angie had run across the street. "And you have your uniform on. Lucy could call the postmaster and get you in trouble."

"I can call my lawyer and get her in trouble." I shook a fist at Lucy from the other side of the glass door, just wishing she'd come out and face me. I pulled up on my tiptoes to look over Angie. "You're a coward! Hiding behind the microphone!"

Angie grabbed me by the arm and tugged me down to my flat feet.

"You've lost your mind. First"—she got really close to me—"you're going around accusing Carla of killing Lee. And secondly, you're trying to start a fistfight with Lucy. What's gotten into you?"

"Carla didn't do it?" I asked as I carefully prepared an argument to tell her why she was wrong.

"I'm holding her for a few hours. But I'm telling you to drop it or I'll have you in jail for interfering with a homicide." Angie didn't bother standing there any longer. "I'm not going to warn you again."

Chapter 12

After I finished my day, I went straight to the diner, where I sought the food I told the front porch ladies I'd grab before I came over to discuss the murder with them at Millie's house. I'd texted my dad earlier to tell him not to take Buster home because I wasn't going right home after work and would pick the dog up after my route.

Mom had made meatloaf for the front porch ladies and me. It smelled so good, and Buster danced around me the entire walk over to Little Creek Road.

"What's that all about?" Mac stood up from the bushes he was clearing in front of his house.

"Not what you think." I nodded toward Millie's house down the road. By the smile on his face, I could tell he thought I was bringing him something to eat. "Your yard looks great."

There was no sense in being mean to him. He was still the same old Mac he'd always been. I just wasn't the woman he thought I was. Besides, I didn't want a relationship with someone who didn't respect who I was, and I wasn't going to change.

"Thanks. Carla said she was giving a final inspection tonight." He laughed.

"Good luck, I hope she doesn't poison you too," I called and didn't look back.

Okay. So it was a little jab about what he called snooping, and maybe I was still a little hurt that he didn't want me, but it was fine. I had the front porch ladies, and probably in the next few years, I'd be one of them. Old. Single. Lonely.

Ugh.

"Get in here," Millie greeted me at the door and rushed me in. "Is that meatloaf?"

"It sure is." I handed it to her.

"I can smell Pat's special meatloaf every time she makes it over there." Millie pointed toward the diner, which was literally right across Little Creek from her house. "Me and the gals have already started doing things like we see detectives on the TV doing."

When I followed her into the kitchen, I saw she wasn't lying. Big sheets of white paper with printed-out photos of Lee, Carla, and Luke were taped on her kitchen wall.

Harriette was busy writing on different-colored sticky notes while Ruby made something on the stove, and Gertrude had her laptop open to social media.

"Welcome to the Front Porch Ladies HQ." Harriette smiled, turning around with a black marker in one hand and a stack of purple stickies in the other. I guess my face said it all. "What? You don't think we know you call us the front porch ladies?"

"I… um…" I stammered.

"Of course we do." Millie put her hands on the sides of my shoulders. "And we love it." She squeezed and then let go. "Now, we don't have time to waste."

"How did you get those photos?" I asked and took my time looking at them.

"Facebook." Harriette looked at me, blinking rapidly and then staring openly. "You don't have Facebook?"

"Would it be a bad thing if I didn't?" I asked.

"Do you know how many fish are in the sea?" Gertrude chimed in. She brought a cup of coffee that just finished percolating over to me.

Was there ever a time they didn't drink coffee or tea? I stared at each of them in awe. They were in such good shape for their ages, and they were on social media.

"You can forget Mac. Honey, I've run across some doozies of men that I'd get my claws into if I were your age." Ruby spread her arms wide. "The World Wide Web is a vast ocean."

"I'm not in the mood for a man, but I am a bit shocked y'all are on Facebook." I couldn't help but think I was the old one here, not the front porch ladies. "But it looks like y'all've done a lot more sleuthing than I have."

"Nah." Harriette's nose curled and put down a plate at each place setting on Millie's table. "We just wanted one of them crime boards you see on the TV. They got them photos of suspects and how come they wanted to murder someone."

While Gertrude, Millie, and Ruby plated all the food and got it ready to put on the table, family style, I looked over their board of suspects. It wasn't too bad.

"You have Carla. I can't help but think she did it." I pointed at a photo they must have had printed because it was awful. It was an unflattering photo of Carla's back side, if you knew what I mean. "You've written her motive was the Make Kentucky Colorful spring campaign as her number-one reason, but I think it goes deeper than that."

Harriette grabbed her ink pen.

"Tell me." She put the pen on the large sheet of paper under Carla's photo.

"First off, I think you're right, but you have to have the evidence to back it up. Not only did Lee die from poisoning—"

Millie let out a little gasp when I mentioned that. Ruby and Gertrude stopped what they were doing and rubbed Millie's back for comfort. I continued, "She has been spraying poison all over Sugar Creek Gap and making all the animals sick."

They wanted to hear every single detail of what Doc Olson had told me about all the sick animals and how she had gone to the beautification meeting to tell Carla to stop. I also mentioned that Carla said at the last meeting that she didn't want to talk ill of the dead but wanted to know when Luke would clean up the house before tomorrow and if she could pay to get someone to do it for him.

Since the story took a little longer than I wanted, Millie had us sit down to eat because she didn't want our supper to get cold. Buster lay under the table near my feet. Every once in a while, I caught Millie glancing at him with a remembering smile on her face.

"Then we have Luke." I looked around while the ladies ate. Millie seemed the most interested in listening instead of eating, but I still told them what I knew between my own bites. "I overheard him at the nursing home talking to Vivian about seeing if Lee qualified for assisted living because he thought Lee was having some dementia."

"He most certainly did not," Millie protested. "He remembered everything. Every last detail of those stamps because trust me, I had to listen and look at them." She let out a long sigh as if it weren't something she really wanted to do. "And he knew what every single box in that house had in it."

"Did he?" I asked.

"Of course he did. He had all his faculties."

I nearly spat out my food when she referred to his senses.

These ladies might be up on their social media, but they sure weren't up on the current terms. Either way, if she knew what was in those boxes, maybe she'd know what was in that negative space, still haunting my memory.

"If I could get us into Lee's house, do you think you could tell me what was in a certain box?" I asked.

"I didn't listen all that well. Did you see all them boxes?" Millie asked with disbelief. "But I guess I could try. Sometimes I dozed off."

"If you claim Lee didn't have a memory problem, then what would be Luke's purpose?" I let the women chew on my question and their food for a couple of minutes before I explained what I'd found out. "Did Lee have money he was leaving to Luke?" I asked. "Money is a great motive to kill someone. Especially when you're broke and desperate and can't pay a regular bill for a visit to the vet for your cat."

"He's broke?" Millie glanced at her friends to see if they were experiencing the same reaction. And they were.

"From what I understand, Luke has been making very small payments on a vet bill for a regular checkup on his cat. If I can recall without looking, it maybe cost me fifty dollars to get Doc Olson to check out Rowena once a year." I left out the heartworm expense, but it wasn't much more than that. "If he can't pay a vet bill, what else can't he pay?"

"Lee said Luke's got a great job, and he's done so well for himself. I never thought otherwise, and since we were just companions, me and Lee," she emphasized, "I never questioned Luke's efforts to get Lee to clean the house, but if he thought he was going to get Lee's stamp collection, he's got another thing coming to him."

"What does that mean?" Ruby asked, leaning a little closer so she could hear with her good ear.

"I'm just saying." Millie had a secret, and her upper stiff lip told me she wasn't about to tell.

"Millie." I decided to change the subject. But if Luke knew Lee wasn't leaving his stamp collection to Luke, then maybe that was another motive to kill. Still, the seed was planted that Luke was one to look out for and they needed keep their ears peeled around their gossip circles, so I moved on. "Did Lee ever say anything about Carla and her threats against him?"

"He brushed her off." Her eyes squinted with a little twinkle of mischief. "He said he loved getting her goat. He said most of the time he'd make the gate screw a little tighter to force her to have to take extra effort to open it. Sometimes he put something extra on the front porch to make her just lose her mind when she drove by." Millie laughed. "She's been driving by and stopping by for the better part of three months."

Harriette had finished eating and was updating the board with all the information I'd given.

"It still didn't give her the right to sneak down there and harass him at night." Millie shook her head and stood up to start collecting the dishes.

I stood up to help her, but she and Gertrude shooed me away and went to go help Harriette with the writing on the paper. Ruby was still eating. She was much slower than the rest of them.

"Who snuck down there at night?" I asked for clarification. "Surely not Carla."

"Surely it was too." The dishes clinked when Millie put them down. "Now that you know me and Lee's secret companionship, I'm not ashamed to say that I would wait for the sun to go down and the night to get real dark out so I could mosey down there for a night cap and not be seen by them nosy old women." Millie picked up another plate to take over to her dishwasher.

"Who you calling nosy?" Ruby asked, jerking up from her plate .

"I'm nosy, but who you calling old?" Gertrude snatched the plate from Millie.

"Anyways, I'd seen Carla park on Short Street at the corner up there and get out of her car with that darn spray bottle. She tiptoed down the banks of Little Creek." She gestured to across the street to the actual creek. "And back up when she got in front of Lee's house." Millie acted like she was squirting something. "She'd spray all around his house. No joke. He knew it because I told him."

"Did you see if she did it the night before I found him?" I asked.

"She sure did. In fact, it was Grand Central Station on Little Creek Road that night." She put her hands on the table and eased herself down in a chair, facing the makeshift suspect board.

"Who else came by?" I asked.

"Luke came by. He and Lee got into some sort of argument, and I couldn't help but hear it from here." She tapped the table.

"You mean from Mac's place, which Walter is trying to sell. Tell her the truth. If she's going to help figure out who killed Lee, she's got to know all the details, Millie." Harriette had reached her limit. "Fine. I'll do it."

"No. It's not your tale to tell, Harriette Pearl." Millie glared at her old friend. "I walked down there when I thought Carla was gone. I didn't realize Luke was there. It was dark, so I didn't see his car." Millie left out the part that she didn't have the best eyes of the group. "When I heard Lee's screen door creak open and heard voices, I knew Lee wasn't alone. So I ran through the gate to the house Mac has for sale and hid on the side next to Lee's house. It was Luke. He and Lee were fussing about something." She blinked a few times as if she couldn't remember.

"Take your time," I encouraged her, because this seemed like important information that might give me reason to believe Luke, not Carla, was the main suspect.

"Well, I don't remember, but he had something in his hand. A box or something." She shook her head.

"Millie, there is a box missing from the stack of boxes, and it is right where I found Lee." I let her know because I needed her to remember what Lee and Luke were arguing about.

"I just can't remember. Oh dear." She put her hand up to her head. "Maybe I'm getting the dementia."

"No, no." Sweet Ruby leaned across and patted Millie's hand, which lay on the table. "You're under a lot of stress. It'll come to you when you need it to."

I needed it to come to her now, but I bit my own lip to keep my mouth shut. With a few of the deep breaths I'd learned from my brief mail stops in Tranquility Wellness, I let it go and moved on.

"So Carla and Luke came by that night." I pointed to the suspect board. "Anyone else?"

"Yes. Walter Ward." Millie threw her hands up in the air. "He's a pickle."

"Did he actually stop in and see Lee or just stop at Mac's house, the one he's selling?" I asked. "I need to know because he and Luke have been seen talking around town. My experience with Walter hasn't been pleasant.

After Richard died, he showed up at the house wanting to know if he could sell it."

"The nerve of that man." Ruby stood up and took her plate over to Gertrude before fixing herself a cup of coffee.

"Lee told Walter to get off his property. He wasn't selling." Millie's lips turned down. "That's when I knew Lee wasn't in no count to have another visitor, and I went home."

"Did you see all of them leave?" I asked.

"I did, but it surely didn't stop them from coming back." Millie pointed at Harriette. "Best put Walter Ward on there too."

The five of us sat there and looked at the board in silence.

"All three had motives. Carla for the hard work and prestige she so desperately wants before she retires at the end of the week. Luke and Walter for the money." I shook my head, then turned to the front porch ladies.

"All three had greed," Harriette said, her eyes darkening.

When I left the front porch ladies after a couple hours of sleuthing and getting a plan, I was full and tired. The plan was that they would keep what little hearing they had open for anyone with clues and I would snoop around on my travels.

Buster was exhausted, too, and it did cross my mind for us to stop at Mac's house. I wanted to let him know that he really opened my eyes and we should probably just be friends, since neither of us wanted to budge on our views, especially his view about me being snoopy. While I was with the ladies, it hit me that I'd rather have Mac as a friend than not at all. Even though we might not be as compatible as we'd hoped, he was still a major player in my family life, and we needed him as much as he needed us.

We didn't stop by his house because his car wasn't in his driveway and his lights were out. He wasn't home. Of course, I wondered all the things—like where was he? Who was he with? What was he doing? Was he with someone, namely a woman?

"Oh geez, Buster." I gripped the wheel of my car on the way out to the farmhouse. "What is wrong with me?"

Buster was lying down in the front passenger seat of the car. He lifted his head and looked up at me with those big brown eyes.

"Why did I suddenly fall hard for him?" I sighed and felt the sadness tingle in my heart. "It wasn't like I planned it. Of course I thought he was a doll when Richard was alive."

Then it struck me. Richard. Why was I still actually thinking Richard and I had a true relationship? I was sure there were more feelings that I needed to explore, and maybe they were what held me back from thinking I could have another relationship with someone. Mac was probably there and convenient.

"I need therapy," I groaned and turned the car into the farmhouse.

There was somewhat of a little drive up the gravel driveway before you could even see my house. It was in desperate need of a gravel refill because the snow from the winter had melted, making some of the gravel slide away. It was very common for this to happen, and Logsdon Landscaping had always done such a nice job that I needed to call Amy.

Then it hit me. I should call Amy Logsdon and see if I could talk to her employees, the ones I had seen drop off the flowers at the house Walter was selling for Mac. Maybe they heard Walter and Lee have some words. Walter was definitely greedy, and I wasn't so sure he was all that innocent.

"Mac." My headlights projected on his car, which sat in front of the farmhouse.

When I pulled up alongside him, he was sitting in the car with his head leaning back on the headrest, and his eyes were closed.

My heart was beating out of my chest when I noticed how cute he looked. Suddenly I realized that I was really sad he didn't want to give me a chance. It made my head spin like I was on some sort of roller coaster with my emotions. Boy, I sure had forgotten how that felt.

Buster and I got out of the car. Mac didn't budge when I slammed the door. Buster ran around the yard to do his business. I walked over to Mac's car and lightly tapped on the window.

His eyes shot open, and his head jerked forward. He looked surprised, as if he were trying to figure out where he was. When he looked at me, he smiled. His face relaxed. His eyes melted me like butter when he looked at me.

"Hey." I nonchalantly greeted him when he opened the door to get out.

"Hey." He shut the door, and what happened next was like some movie. He literally grabbed me, bringing his body to mine and planting the biggest kiss I'd ever gotten in my life.

You know those kisses. They're the kind you've been anticipating for a long time and when they finally happen, they are so much better than you'd planned.

"I've been doing a lot of thinking today," he whispered, cradling my head to his chest and stroking my hair.

I was sure I stank. I'd been walking around all day with that big mail bag, and trust me when I said I sweat. Every night I took a shower when I got off work, but I'd yet to be home.

"I tried to be mad that you'd even want to help figure out who killed Lee, but what I was really mad at was the fact I've been wanting this for a long time." As he talked, I could feel his heart pounding in his chest up against my ear. The more he talked, the more closely he held me. "I was mad at myself for thinking of Richard and how he'd feel. One time I confronted him about her." Mac didn't have to mention her name for me to know it was the woman Richard had the relationship with the entire time we were married. "I told him you were too good for him. He knew. He knew I was attracted to you, and he laughed at me."

I pulled away and looked at him. The moon was bright and shining down on us. The edges of his eyes dipped.

"He laughed?" I asked.

"He said that you'd never believe me if I told you about her and that I'd never get you from him." His jaw tensed. "He punched me."

As if time stood still, I quickly remembered coming home from Grady's practice when Mac had a massive nosebleed.

"Was it the night..." I brought the memory to life.

"Yeah." Mac ran his hand down my hair. "Over the past twenty-four hours, I let Richard in my head. I think it was easier for me to blame you for wanting to put your life in danger for looking into a murder case than to be rejected by you."

"Why don't you let me decide that?" I reached up and took his hand in mine, leading him into the house with Buster alongside us. Inside, we were greeted by a very excited Rowena.

Chapter 13

"Shhh." I put my finger up to my mouth as I walked into my family room with a cup of early morning coffee in my hand.

Rowena was sitting on the top of the couch in her queen pose and greeting me for the morning. Really, she was telling me she was ready to eat, and she was going to tell me about it.

In the pre-Buster days, Rowena would run to her bowl and meow until I, the automatic feeder, filled her bowl with kibble. Now it seemed as if she were trying to figure out how this new intruder worked in the grand scheme of our feeding ritual. Since it was still too early for her feeder to go off and I'd gotten a cup of coffee, she must've thought it was time to eat.

"I know, I know." I looked down the hall, where Mac and Buster were sleeping. "I've totally disrupted our cozy little twosome." I sat down on the couch and stroked her, finishing up with a little finger rub.

Her purr told me I was forgiven. Last night with Mac was exactly what I needed. Long kisses and meaningful conversations about how we were breaking ourselves free of the hold Richard had on us were better than any therapy session I could've had. Both of us cried over the relationship we thought we had with Richard, and we even reminisced about the good times we'd had with him. Believe it or not, there were good times.

Though our new relationship would be based on us and not Richard, we did discuss how Grady was Richard's son and Grady loved his father deeply, even though he knew about Richard's other relationship. We'd decided how, going forward, we would be respectful of Richard's memory when it came to Grady.

"I've got to get to work." I took a few sips of my coffee and listened in for any sort of movement from the bedroom. "It must be nice to own your own company," I told Rowena just as her feeder went off. She bolted off the couch and into the kitchen.

Next to the kitchen was the laundry room. Luckily, I didn't have to go back to my room to get dressed in my uniform because I let my uniforms hang dry after they went through the wash cycle. Grady's bedroom contained a private bathroom, which I kept fully stocked in case he and Julia wanted to spend the night.

Before I headed into his bathroom to grab a quick shower, I pulled out some of the breakfast scones Iris and I had made a few weeks ago from the freezer and set them out to thaw.

When I finished getting ready, there was still no movement in the house. Rowena had filled her belly, and she was lying on her back on the top rung of her cat tree in the family room. I quickly scribbled a note to Mac and left it next to the scones.

I left him the directions on how to heat the scone to perfection and to flip on the coffee pot because I started brewing him a fresh pot of coffee. When I was about to sign my name, I hesitated because I wasn't sure how to end it, so I simply wrote a B for my initial.

Today was a day I'd been dreading for the past few months. It was the Make Kentucky Colorful campaign's judging day, the big day Carla had been waiting for. Oddly, I found myself in a pretty good mood on my drive into the post office, where I found Monica putting the battery-operated lights on the LLV in the parking lot.

"You look awfully chipper." Monica must've noticed the glow on my face. "You do know what today is, right? And how you need to string the lights on the mail cart?"

"Mmm-hhhhmm," I said with a nod and headed to the building, where I needed to get started on the lights. "It's going to be a great day," I called over my shoulder, leaving her with a stunned look.

I rarely used the mail cart, but today I was able to get all three loops of my mail in it so I didn't have to keep coming back to the post office between my stops. It would make for a smoother day, and maybe I'd be able to see Mac again tonight.

Plus I would have a little more time to snoop around since I didn't have to come back here to pick up more mail. Ultimately, I needed to snoop around.

"What on earth do you have there?" Vince Caldwell was sitting on the front porch of the main building of the nursing home, where he loved to have his morning coffee and look at the paper or work on his crossword. "I didn't know what that was coming this way when I saw it."

It was still pretty dark out when I made my way over to the nursing home with the light flashing around the cart.

"Carla." I rolled my eyes. "Speaking of which, did you find anything out from your contact?" I sorted through the mail to grab his little stack of mail. Then I suddenly noticed a few pieces of mail that looked the same in various customers' stacks. I took a quick peek and noticed it was the much-anticipated invitation to Zeke's grand-daughter-in-law-to-be's bridal shower.

Boy, were the front porch ladies going to be happy—and that would make Carla happy too.

"I checked out Carla first. Spotless record. She should've been a nun." He grinned. "I also had them look into Walter Ward. Though he's pretty shady on how he gets his properties, and from what I found out around here, when someone comes in here and needs to sell their home so they can pay to live here, Walter is the first one to approach them. So when you said you saw him talking to Luke, I'm thinking Luke had contacted Walter."

"Okay." I was confused. "What do you make of all that?"

"I got the coroner's report." He pulled a piece of paper from the guts of his newspaper and handed it to me.

My jaw dropped when I opened it and saw it was Lee's final autopsy report.

"How on earth did you get this?"

"I told you I had my contacts." He tapped the paper. "According to the autopsy, Lee died of rat poisoning, which weed killer doesn't have, and the sheriff let Carla go."

"Rat poisoning," I gasped, knowing Mac told Walter to get rid of the problem.

Did Walter think the problem Mac was talking about was Lee?

"I've got to go." I grabbed the handle and waved the piece of paper in the air. "Thank you!"

This was amazing news. As much as I'd figured Carla had done it, the report clearly stated it was rat poison, and the only person I saw with rat poison was Walter Ward.

"Mac." I had dialed him with my free hand on my way

back to Main Street, where I was going to deliver to the shops. "Are you awake? Of course you're not awake."

"Good morning." His husky, sleepy voice made my heart fall. "I'm sitting here with a nice cup of fresh coffee you brewed with Rowena in my lap and Buster at my feet."

"Listen." Now that I knew he was awake, I had to tell him. "Remember when you told Walter Ward to get rid of the problem?"

"What problem?" he asked.

"The problem of why your house next to Lee's isn't selling." I had to take this information to Angie.

"Oh, the rats?" he asked like he needed confirmation.

"You meant the rats. I think Walter thinks you meant Lee himself." The facts were the facts, and I couldn't wait to tell the front porch ladies.

"Huh?" he asked uncertainly. "I'm not sure if I've ever talked to you this early, but I'm feeling like you need more coffee."

"Mac, I'm serious. I found out Lee had died from rat poison, not weed poison." Even though I heard him let out a long, deep sigh, I continued and tugged on the handle of the cart. After crossing Main Street to stop into Social Knitwork, I got stuck going over the curb. "When you told Walter to get rid of the problem, the problem he thought was Lee because he said that's where the rats were coming from. What if he did stop the problem, meaning Lee, then he met with Luke because he knew Luke would be the heir to Lee's stuff?"

"First off, Lee doesn't have any stuff worth having, from what I can tell." He clearly didn't know about the stamps. "Secondly, Walter is not an idiot. He knew I meant the rats on my property."

"I can't discount the argument Lee and Walter had when I was there, and Walter is very greedy. If he thought he was going to lose a deal, you never know what he could do." It was a fact.

I left the cart outside and headed inside to see if Leotta had any outgoing mail.

"None today," I told her when I came in empty handed. She waved and went right back to the class she was already teaching.

"None what?" Mac asked.

"Oh, I'm on my route." It was all I had to say for him to know I wasn't talking to him. "Seriously. Think about it." A deep, gratified sigh escaped me. "The fact is that he was poisoned with rat poison. The only person…"

"What? What's wrong?" Mac asked with urgency.

"Mac," I said with a gasp. "What if Walter did do it and he is brought in by Angie and he tells her that you told him to get rid of the problem? And you paid him, didn't you?"

"Yeah. I paid him to get rid of the rats."

"I'm worried. I better not tell Angie." My stomach felt empty all of a sudden.

I grabbed the little bit of mail for Tranquility Wellness and walked in. Some sort of gong class was going on, so I left the mail on the counter and slipped right back out the door.

"Tell Angie?" Mac asked but continued, "See. This right here. I told you I couldn't take you getting involved again. You should be enjoying your day and not worrying about Lee Macum and what the sheriff is doing to solve it."

"I'm worried that you're going to be pegged as the killer and Walter Ward would point a finger at you." I recalled, "Remember when the church was selling off part of their land to help pay off the new building? Walter had originally agreed to do it for free. Doing it for God, he said.

But when it came down to it and the land went into a bidding war, he took the cut above what was originally the asking price. Saying it was God's way of paying him back for doing a good deed." Even thinking about that still put a bad taste in my mouth.

"That man is a disgrace to our town, and he killed Lee Macum!" I didn't figure my voice to be so loud when I walked into the Wallflower Diner.

Everyone turned around to look at me just as I came nose to nose with Carla.

Chapter 14

"Who killed him?" Carla stood solidly at the ready.

"Umm…" My brows furrowed. "I'll call you back."

I hung up the phone and slipped it into the pockets of my uniform.

"I want to know who killed him because I'm going to kill them." She wagged a gardening spade at me. "Do you know what it's like to be locked up in jail for twenty-four hours when you didn't do something? Do you know what it's like to be accused and shamed by all the people of your town when all I've ever done was give back to all of y'all?" She dragged that spade around the room while she moved with it, eyeballing all the customers in the diner.

"You better watch what you say about killing some-one," I leaned in to whisper. "That might've been what got you in trouble the first time—that and the fact you were spraying poison weed killer on anything blowing in the wind."

Carla did look a little disheveled, and she even had on the same clothes as she did yesterday.

"When did you get out of the poky?" I teased, only to find she wasn't very accepting of it.

"Not funny, Bernadette." She looked around my shoulder. Everyone in the diner seemed to have gone back to gossiping about Lee. "I'm glad to see you have the cart lit up. Have you noticed how nice the town looks this morning?"

I was happy to see she had forgotten about what I'd said to Mac when I was walking into the diner. The last thing I wanted was for the spotlight to be turned on Mac as the mastermind behind Walter's evil deed.

"Of course. We are going to win, and I've got a smile on my face today too." I smiled real big so she didn't tell me how to act like she tried to do to Lee. "I've got to be on my way."

I maneuvered around the tables of the diner and made it back to the counter, where my mom exchanged her stack of mail for a box of pancakes and sausage.

"I heard Mac didn't come home last night. So I figured you better leave this for him at the office." Mom gave me a onceover. "Do you figure you should be getting yourself into something?"

"Mom." My jaw dropped. "I'm fifty years old."

"And your age makes me any less of your mother?" She gave me an alert gaze.

"Mom, I…"

She interrupted and wanted to be the first one to speak of it.

"Your daddy and I want the best for you and the companion you choose to spend your life with." She started in on all that companion talk.

"Mom." I put my hand up to stop her. "I don't want a companion. I want a man. A man that's going to be my best friend and …"

"Lalalala." Grady appeared behind me and had his fingers in his ears. "Is all this talk over?" he asked in a really loud voice, fingers still plugging his hearing.

Mom and I both laughed.

"Listen, Grandma." Grady took the cup of coffee waiting by the register. "I'm all for Mom living a life with Mac if that's what makes her happy, but I'm telling both y'all now." He looked down at us before he set his eyes on me. "If you two don't work out, I'm still going to have him in my life as normal."

"Hey." Mac walked up. He looked at me and smiled. He hesitated and then leaned over and kissed me right then and there… on the lips. "Good morning," he said to everyone else and shook Grady's hand like normal.

All of us kind of stood there, a little shocked, since it wasn't Mac's way of greeting me or any of us.

"What?" He looked from me to Mom to Grady. "It's not like y'all don't know about me and Bernie." He put his hand on the small of my back and gave it a little scratch on top of my coat. "Right?"

And just like that… Mac went in for another kiss.

"Here." I shoved the box of pancakes and sausage between us to give a little space.

"I was sending it next door to you because I knew you had to come in soon, since Julia is going to the doctor." My mom took pride in making sure Mac knew feeding him was all her idea. "And you're gonna need your strength to put up with her," she joked with Mac.

"Are you kidding?" Mac looked at me, and my knees went weak. "I've been dying to know what it's like to put up with her, and I've got to say that it's pretty amazing."

"Geez." Grady rolled his eyes. "I'm outta here." He gave Mac a hug and another one to me before giving my mom the final kiss on the cheek.

"Why are you so late to work?" I asked Grady, but he was already halfway through the diner, and the chit-chat was too loud for him to hear me. "Julia not better?"

"She called me telling me she was going to be late, so I made sure Rowena and Buster were okay before I left to come to work." He lifted the box up to his nose and inhaled. He smiled, making my mom's face light up with joy. She loved when people enjoyed her cooking. "I'll go let Buster out at lunch."

"Okay." I could get used to this feeling I was having, but the ringing from my phone brought me right out of it.

"Who is it?" Mac asked me when I looked at it and paused.

"Tim Crouse." I wondered why a lawyer was calling me. "I better get it. I'll see y'all later."

This time I initiated the kiss between Mac and me, leaving him with the biggest smile I'd ever seen on him.

"Hey, Tim. What's up?" I asked as I nestled the phone between my shoulder and ear and picked up the handle to the cart.

"Bernadette, I'm Lee Macum's attorney, and there's a request that you be at the hearing of the will this morning." Tim's words forced me to stop in mid-stride, causing the cart to run up on my heels.

"Ouch," I gasped.

"Are you okay?" Tim asked from the other end of the phone.

"Yeah. I guess I'm not sure why I'd need to be at the will reading." Then it dawned on me. "Buster," I whispered.

Lee had given me Buster in his will. Now the entire thing with me being the emergency contact made sense.

"Sure." I didn't bother waiting to see what Tim's

response to me questioning my being there had to do with me. "What time?" I asked.

"Can you come now?" he asked with a little hesitation. "Luke is here, and we'd like to start."

"I'm right across the street at the diner. I'll quickly deliver the rest of the shops over on this side of Main Street then head right over." I put the phone back in my pocket.

This was about the only time I was glad to be pulling the cart. Normally the courthouse, which was where Tim's attorney's office was located, was on my last mail route. With the mail already with me, I could just pull out all the mail from the offices in the courthouse and deliver it before I went over to Little Creek Road.

Our courthouse was located right behind the mill wheel and housed all the officially elected offices, clerks' offices, PVA, and much more. Most of the lawyers in town even rented office space there. The sheriff department was in the back, and the volunteer fire department was located in the building next to the back parking lot. It was a one-stop legal shop for all of Sugar Creek Gap. The Sugar Creek Gap Library was located next to the courthouse, followed by the funeral home, which would be my next stops. I hoped I could snoop a little by asking Jigs Baker some questions about Lee's autopsy.

"You're early," Trudy Evans greeted me from behind her computer where she worked in the clerk's office. "My computer says it's ten o'clock."

"You're right. I've got a will reading in Tim's office, so I figured I'd drop this off right here." Normally, I wouldn't discuss anything around Trudy that I wouldn't want the whole entire world to know, but I did want people to know so I could get them talking. I needed the gossip that it would generate so I could get more insight into who really asked questions, which I hoped would lead me to the killer. Or, at least, if Walter Ward knew I was getting Buster, maybe he'd come find me. Then I could question him. Either way, me telling Trudy about the will was a manipulated move.

"Will reading?" She looked around her computer and stood up as if she were really interested in the stack of mail bound by a rubber band.

"Mm-hmmm." I pinched my lips together, giving her a slow nod, happy she took my bait. I leaned in real far over the tall counter between us and whispered like it was some big secret, "Lee Macum's will."

"For shame." Trudy drew a hand to her chest. "Is that what's going on up there? I seen Luke come in with Walter. Up the stairs they went." She flung her hand in the air when she mentioned the location of Tim's office. "I seen it because I was getting me a refill on coffee. No sooner did I make it to the clerk's door to unlock it than did Walter hurry right back down spittin' all sorts of curse words." She glanced right and then left. "I heard Luke had all but signed over Lee's house to Walter."

"You mean as in to sell?" You could never be too sure what Trudy heard. She liked to add a little flair to things.

"Oh no. As in letting Walter buy the house from him." She took a hard swallow and dipped her chin when someone walked by. "Luke is having a hard time paying his property taxes. You know it's that time of the year, and the city has already given him an extension."

My phone chirped, and I pulled it out of my pocket.

"Gotta go." I wagged the phone. "Tim is hurrying me up."

"Bernadette." Trudy stopped me before I headed out the door. "I hear you and Mac…" She gave me a theatrical wink. "There just might be something to celebrate."

Yep… she added a little flair to that.

I gave a simple wave, knowing my not denying what she heard would only add fuel to her gossip, even though Mac and I had no plans to solidify the relationship. When I headed up the steps to Tim's office, I noticed Walter was sitting on one of the benches on the bottom floor. He was too busy on his phone for him to recognize me, but I knew for sure he was waiting for Luke.

What Trudy told me was a hard pill to swallow and it might not be all true, but it sure did look like Walter was on edge about something. And if what she did tell me wasn't gossip and Walter did buy the house from Luke, it would take months to finish out the paperwork. Poor Lee's body probably wasn't even cold yet.

"Bernie, come on in." Tim noticed me at his office door and waved me in. "I'm sure you two know each other." Tim gestured between us from his chair behind his desk.

"Oh yeah." Luke stood up from one of the two chairs in front of Tim's desk. He gave me a hug. "How is Buster?"

"He's great. He's fitting in just fine at the old farmhouse." Among other people, I still felt a giddiness inside about Mac and Buster being new to Rowena and me.

"Well, let's get started." Tim looked at Luke. "Luke, if you don't mind waiting outside, that'd be great."

"What?" Luke gave a snorting laugh.

"I need to talk to Bernadette alone first." Tim got up, walked around his desk, and then held the door open for Luke. "I'll be with you shortly."

"I don't understand." Luke was puzzled.

"You will," Tim assured him and ushered him out the door. He shut it behind Luke. "Bernadette, you and I've been friends a long time. I'm sure what I'm about to tell you is going to floor you in some way."

"What? You're making me nervous." I tried to swallow, but my mouth had become dry.

"According to Lee Macum's last will and testament, he's made you the beneficiary of his entire estate. That includes his stamp collection, his house, his dog, and everything inside."

"Come again?" I asked in a shaky, soft, halting, disbelieving voice.

"I said—"

I raised my hand to cut Tim off.

"I heard what you said. What about..." I couldn't for the life of me remember the name of the man who was just there. I haphazardly pointed to the door.

"He left him nothing. Well, he left him a penny." Tim eased down on the desk right in front of me and sat on the edge. He folded his hands at his waist and looked at me. "Are you okay?"

"I'm not sure why." I blinked in bafflement.

"You were kind to him." Tim reached back and grabbed an envelope from his desk.

When he handed it to me, I noticed my name was written on the front in Lee's handwriting. I knew it well from delivering and taking his mail from him for ten years.

"I'm sure his note will explain it all." Tim smiled. "Don't worry about Luke. He's going to take it hard, but it's all yours."

Tim stood up and grabbed a big manila envelope and handed it to me. Without looking, I could tell there were keys in it, probably to Lee's house.

There were a few things to sign, and Tim told me all about the legal system and how it all worked. Lee's assets were frozen. I needed a death certificate for any accounts, but all Tim's words ran together as my mind still tried to process what was happening.

"If you have any questions, you know I'm a phone call away." He walked my zombie-like body to the door.

Luke didn't bother letting me out first. He ran in and took a seat.

"Now I've got to deal with him." Tim winked and smiled before shutting the door in my face.

The sound crinkling of the manila envelope brought me back to earth as I gripped it. I looked down. One hand had the letter, and the other had Lee's things. I'd not seen either coming.

Yelling came from the other side of Tim's door. I knew I had better get out of there before I become the next victim after this bizarre death of Lee Macum.

Chapter 15

"You knew, didn't you?" I gave Millie a hard look when I delivered her mail.

The front porch ladies weren't on their porches by Carla's strike orders. She had told them the judges only wanted to judge houses, and they didn't make the front porches pretty. Yes. They took offense, and I was sure there were some ugly words between them, but ultimately, Carla won.

I had to deliver their mail to their front doors with very little chit-chat except when I got to Millie's.

"You even mentioned something the other day, and you were talking about Lee leaving it all to me." I recalled that Millie had acted a little aloof when I questioned her the other night over supper.

"I swore to Lee I wouldn't say a word, but now that you know…" She grabbed me and tugged me to come into the house. "I do think Luke killed him and not Carla."

"Since you ladies haven't been on the porch, you've not heard." I had stepped inside and followed her to the kitchen. The paper we'd written on was still there. "Carla is out of jail because it came back that Lee was killed with rat poison."

"Walter." Her eyes lowered. She walked over to the paper and picked up the Sharpie marker. She popped off the top and ran a line through Carla's name. "He's been dying to get his hands on all of these houses on this block, even the ones Mac has down there."

"Is that right?" I asked.

"Speaking of Mac." A big smile crossed her thin lips. "I did hear he didn't come home last night."

"Harriette Pearl has a big mouth," I said, blushing. "And she's right."

"Good for you." Millie went back to the paper and circled Walter's name. "Lee didn't like him. He said he was a bad seed, and if he got his hands on a house here, he'd turn it all into some sort of retail."

"Is that why Lee gave me the house?" I asked.

"Did you read the letter?" She knew about it too.

"Not yet. I thought I'd wait until after I was safe in my own home tonight," I told her. "But I am going to go down there and let myself in so I can get a good look around. There's the one thing that has bothered me about Lee's death."

"There are many things..." Millie's voice trailed off as she looked at something on the horizon.

It was the space on the bottom of the pile of boxes where something had gone that really bothered me.

"When you feel up to it, I'd like for you to come down there and see if you could remember what was in that empty spot I told you about." I didn't want to rush her, but something really nagged at me. "What about Lee's stamp collection? Do you know where that is?"

"Oh honey. It's like a needle in a haystack in there. It'll take you months to go through that house." She and I walked to the door just in time to see Carla's car zooming past on her way down the street towards Lee's house.

"I better get going before she sends out the troops to figure out why I abandoned my cart." I walked out of Millie's house.

"Have you seen any of the judges?" Millie asked.

"Nope. Not a one." I shrugged and made my way off her porch and out of her gate.

Carla was standing in front of Lee's house, her hands on her hips and her toes tapping. The wheels on my cart squeaked, and her head jerked up.

"Just the woman I wanted to see." She bolted toward me with her hand still stuck on her hips. "I heard something. I heard you were the owner of this here house now."

"Yes, ma'am I sure am." I no longer had any reason to deny it. I was sure the word had spread quickly after Luke found out.

"Then I need you to stop delivering that mail." She tried to jerk the handle of the cart away from me.

"Carla, stop it." I gripped the handle tighter. "This is property of the government, and you cannot handle such a piece of equipment."

"A cart? I certainly can." She tried to grab it again, and when she didn't succeed, she tried to get in it.

"Carla! Stop it!" I shooed her away. "This is ridiculous. I have a job to do."

"And I have a job to do." She moved herself between the gate and me. "I want you to clean up that porch right now before the judges get here."

A very slow-moving car stopped in front of the house, and we both looked at it. Two people sat in the front seat, and two people sat in the back. They held up clipboards and eyed Lee's house, making notes on their paper.

"Oh my stars!" Carla waved them to roll down their window. "Are you the judges?"

One of them confirmed with a quiet yes along with a nod.

"He just died, and we are here to clean up!" She turned back to me, unlatched the gate with one hand, and shoved me into the yard. "Can you come back and check?" She continued to push me up the sidewalk.

"You've lost your mind," I said through my gritted teeth and planted smile.

It was apparent she wouldn't take no for an answer.

"Shush up and get me in this house." She grabbed a few things from the front porch while I got the key out of the manila envelope. "Oh my gawd," Carla growled.

Both of us stood there stiff as boards, huddled up. Truly, there were boxes everywhere in the entrance. Carla didn't have even a half inch to put down whatever it was she'd brought in from the porch.

"I'll… umm…" She shoved it into my arms and simply turned around to go grab something else from outside. "Go find a place for it," she barked at me, and I did.

When I came in here the other morning and found Lee, I guess I was on such a mission to find him that I didn't even begin to look around at just how bad it really was in here. It was like a corn maze, only with boxes. They were stacked in columns from the bottom of the floor to the ceiling. When I got to the split in the path, I decided to go right, since I remembered going left into the family room where I'd found him.

The path to the right led to a kitchen. It wasn't nearly as bad as rest of the house. It wasn't a dirty house, just a very cluttered one. In fact, the kitchen was very clean, and only a few boxes sat on top of the kitchen table. There weren't any dishes in the sink. When I opened the kitchen cabinets, the dishes were stacked up nice and neatly. Even Buster's bowls had nice dog mats under them, and they were shiny clean. It was nice to see that Lee had somewhat taken care of Buster's eating needs.

"Why did you have so many boxes?" I asked Lee as if he were in the room and could hear me. I set the item Carla had given me from the front porch, which looked to be a broken flower vase, down on the table and decided it was a good time to see if there was any rat poison to be found in the kitchen. Obviously the sheriff's department had already scoured the place for anything before they cleared it, but it was always possible for them to have overlooked something.

I looked in all the cabinets, including underneath the kitchen sink, but only the usual was under there—dish soap along with a dish rack and some scrub brush items as well as some garbage bags.

"I honestly can't believe he lived like this." Carla had found me in the kitchen looking under the sink. "Give me one of them garbage bags."

She zeroed in on those.

"If I were you, I'd get that boy toy of yours over here with a bulldozer and give it a few good swipes." She gave a hard nod and disappeared back into the maze of boxes.

When I heard her go out the front door, which I guess she did to collect the trash, I plucked a garbage bag from the box and decided to walk into the room where I'd found Lee. The room was nothing like I had remembered it. It was much more open with just the stack of boxes along one side of the wall.

I couldn't help myself. I opened a few of the boxes to see the contents inside. Some had what looked like knick-knacks he might've picked up from his trash-collecting days, while others were empty, and still others had what looked like trash.

"No stamps?" I questioned, remembering all the stamps I'd given him over the last ten years. I couldn't believe the dozen or so boxes I'd quickly looked through. "At least one of the boxes should have a stamp," I said, feeling my forehead wrinkle.

I saw a small couch and a recliner facing a television with a coffee table. Lee must have been sitting in the recliner because it was closest to where I'd found him. If I did recall correctly, it had appeared as if he'd tried to stand and then fell to the floor.

My eyes shifted to the boxes, specifically the spot where something was clearly missing. I took my phone out of my back pocket and took a photo of the missing box. I figured, if anything, I could show Millie and see if she remembered something being there.

"What is that?" I noticed something in the far back of the empty space. Careful not to touch the surrounding boxes in fear I'd hit one and create an avalanche I might not survive, I reached in slowly.

"What are you doing down there?" Carla's voice boomed.

"I'm picking up trash." I grabbed an empty coffee cup from The Roasted Bean, a little disappointed that it wasn't some major clue because Lee did love going to talk to Matilda Garrison, the young owner of the downtown coffee shop.

"Give me that." Carla grabbed it from me and shoved it in her bag of trash, which she knotted it at the top. "I've done the best I can to get up all the trash. Now, you need to call Amy Logsdon right now to get in here and put around some potted plants. There's not much we can do to get the place painted out there or I would, so we are going to have to make do with what we got." She gave me a stern look. "Bernadette, are you listening to me?"

"Yes, Carla." I wanted to ask her. Even though she didn't kill Lee—or like him—did she not feel one once of sadness from his passing?

"Well? What are you waiting for?" She nudged me.

I pretended to scroll through my phone and hit the call key, acting as if I were going to call Amy, which I wasn't. I actually called Mac.

"Hey, it's Bernie. I wanted to let you know Lee Macum had made me beneficiary of his will, leaving everything to me." I could hear him gasping and trying to say something, but I kept talking. "Carla and I are here trying to make the outside of the house a little more presentable, and she wanted me to call you, Amy Logsdon, to see if you can send some colorful potted plants over to sit around outside to brighten up the place."

"Give me the phone." Carla tried to grab my cell from me, and I smacked her hand away.

"Lee left you his house? That mess?" Mac had caught on to what I was doing. "Carla is nuts. I can't wait to hear about how this whole thing came about, but more importantly, I'm dying to see you. What if I meet you at the post office after work and we head on over to the diner for the ceremony together?"

"Perfect." My heart beat so fast in my chest. I couldn't believe I was feeling this way. Even though my entire marriage to Richard was a lie, it felt good to have these feelings when I thought I'd never have them again.

My phone beeped in another call.

"I have to go. I'm getting a call from the funeral home. They probably need me to pick up a package." Mac and I said a quick goodbye, and then I clicked over. "Hey, Jigs. I'll be over soon. Do you need me to come in the office?"

"Actually, Bernie, I'm calling because Lee's body is ready to be released by the sheriff." Jigs caught me off guard.

"Body? Huh?" I gulped when it hit me that I was the beneficiary of everything, including Lee and what was to come next. "Oh."

"There were arrangements made by Luke Macum, but seeing how he doesn't have the authority to do that, I'm kinda in a pickle here." Jigs sounded baffled.

"What were the plans?" I asked, moving slightly away from Carla when she stuck her head up to mine, trying to listen.

"Luke was having a viewing ceremony tomorrow at ten a.m., then a repass at his house after. He stopped by after the reading of the will and mentioned he'd still like to keep the arrangements if you wanted to."

"He did?" I asked, thinking it would be fine with me.

"Mm-hmm, now he'd not be responsible for paying for it, you understand." It was Jigs's way of letting me know the bill was on my shoulders.

"Of course." I sucked in a deep breath. "I'll call Luke and make sure, so if you don't hear from me, we can just plan on the viewing being tomorrow. What about Lee's clothes?" I wondered if I needed to get some clothes from Lee's closet for his viewing.

"Luke already took care of all that," Jigs said, taking me a little off guard.

Luke had seemed to have it all taken care of and in such a little amount of time.

"Okay. I'll talk to him. Thanks for letting me know." I hung up the phone.

"What was that about?" Carla's eyes lowered.

"If you do me a favor, I'll make sure the front of the house is amazing." I was willing to make a deal.

"What's the catch? The favor?" she asked in a slow uneasy tone.

"Tonight at the award ceremony and your retirement ceremony, I want you to make the announcement about Lee Macum's funeral arrangements and repass tomorrow." Being nice would be a hard pill for her to swallow, since she'd been accused of killing him.

"Deal." She stuck her hand out for me to shake. "But didn't you already call Amy?"

What Carla didn't know wouldn't hurt her.

Chapter 16

I had made good on my promise. After Carla and I left Lee's house, I called Amy Logsdon, delivered the rest of my route, and waited to call Luke on my way back. When I did, I told him who I was, since I was sure he didn't have my number.

"I've been waiting to see if you were going to call me," Luke said.

"I'm sorry, Luke. I honestly had no idea Lee had put me in his will." There was no easy way around it.

"Put you in it?" He scoffed. "He gave it all to you. The woman who had to be nice to him six days a week for what, ten minutes a day? An hour a week."

"Listen, I know this is hard for you, but I truly had no idea, and I'm happy to give you anything you'd like." It spilled out of my mouth.

"No matter what you say or offer, it doesn't negate the fact that my uncle had no idea what it took for me to come see him and how much influence he had on me in collecting stamps. I only started to collect them to have something in common with the man." There was such a bitterness in his voice, I knew there was no way he would be levelheaded and listen to me.

"Trust me, I'm as shocked as you are, and fighting about it over the phone won't get us anywhere." I was trying to be calm and cool about it. "I understand you talked to Jigs Baker about his funeral and offered to still keep it as you had planned."

When I heard him babbling and stammering on the other end of the phone, I knew he was going to bellyache about the cost, so I headed him off at the pass.

"If you want to keep it the same, I'm more than happy to do your wishes and foot the bill." That stopped him from groaning.

"You mean have the funeral tomorrow and the repass at my house?" he questioned.

"Yes. That's exactly what I mean." I had finally made it back to the post office parking lot and none too soon. Mac was pulling up. "After the dust has settled, you and I can sit down to talk about Lee's stuff and if there's anything you'd like from his home."

I still wasn't convinced he didn't kill his uncle.

"Just in time." I hung up the phone and flipped off the lights. "And glad to get rid of this thing."

"You are so adorable in your outfit." Mac touched my nose.

"You know, I really like the romantic Mac more than the friend Mac." I couldn't stop myself. It was like there was some sort of pull from his lips to mine when we were around each other. I curled up on my toes and kissed him.

"I like girlfriend Bernie way better than friend Bernie." He pulled me closer, sealing his words.

"Geez, is this what I've got to look at when we are all together?" Grady and Julia had walked up.

"What are you two doing here?" I looked between them.

"Julia had a doctor's appointment." Grady put an arm around her.

"Oh no. I hope they figured out what's wrong." I couldn't believe she'd been going to the doctor for a better part of three days straight and she still looked pale.

"We thought the fresh air walking to the doctor's appointment would do me good." Julia smiled. "Looks like nothing is going to do good until nine months are up."

"Nine months?" I tried to think of any sickness that would take nine months. "Nine months!"

"Yes." Grady and Julia smiled widely.

"Oh my God!" I screamed. "I'm going to be a grandmother!"

I threw my arms around them both, squeezing them as tightly as I could.

"I'm so sorry." I jerked away once I realized I was hugging Julia so tight that I might be inadvertently suffocating my grandchild. "Oh my." I started to cry. "My baby is having a baby."

"Mom." Grady hugged me. "Don't cry."

"It's not sadness. I'm so thrilled for you two and for me." I patted him on the back as he held me. "You two are going to be fantastic parents."

"We were going to wait and tell you at Sunday supper, but I guess Grady saw you and just exploded." Julia's tone was so happy.

"Congratulations, man." Mac put his hand out to shake Grady's.

"Handshake?" Grady laughed. "When did we get so formal?"

The two men hugged and embraced each other. I even thought I saw Mac wipe away a tear, but I wasn't going to bring it up. I knew Mac loved Grady as much as I loved Grady. He was there for Grady's birth, and now he would be a big part of Grady's child's life, no matter what our future held.

I let the three of them talk while I ran the mail cart inside and changed into some regular clothes that I'd kept in my locker at the post office. While I was in there, I opened the letter Lee had written me.

Dear Bernadette,

I wanted to thank you for the years you've been kind to me. You went above and beyond the duty of delivering my mail. On countless occasions when I wasn't feeling well, you were kind to me by bringing me biscuits and soup, not to mention the coffee, to help brighten my day. You have been so kind to my little buddy, Buster, that it was only fitting to have him live with you. As for my house, well, you never complained about having to step over anything I deemed to be a treasure. You do know that when I worked for the garbage company, I did find delight in taking others' trash home for a treasure. After all, we all need a home, and one man's trash is my treasure. My home is no castle, but I figured one day that you and my neighbor up the road would get together and you might want to move out of that lonely farmhouse way on the outskirts of town. Maybe you should give that to your boy so he and his wife can raise their family there. Just a thought.

Regardless, I find you a very kind soul. Not that my nephew Luke isn't a good boy, but he only cares about money, and I have no doubt he'll be just fine without me. Not that I don't think you'll be fine, but I kind of reckon I feel like I ought to take care of you as you have of me. And you see fit to whatever you want to do with my belongings.

I have a very rare stamp that I've been meaning to sell. I've been in contact with a philatelist for years about it. I've not pulled the trigger on selling it quite yet as I'm writing you this letter. But I've left his business card in the envelope for you to contact. I reckon the stamp is worth a lot of money, and I reckon you could use it, seeing you're single and all.

I couldn't stop smiling. I could hear Lee's voice as I read the letter. He went on to say how he really appreciated me and hoped I'd one day make something of what he left me and not squander it on something silly. I folded the card up and put it back in the envelope. I also took out the business card of Isiah Blackwell, the philatelist.

I decided to make a quick call.

"Hi, Isiah. My name is Bernadette Butler," I said into the voicemail. "I am the beneficiary of Lee Macum, and he left your name to call about a stamp. I'm not really sure what type of stamp I'm looking for in Lee's home. So I'd appreciate a call back so we can discuss this further."

I put the phone in my jean pocket and headed back out to meet the rest of my group so we could hurry over to the diner to hear if Sugar Gap Creek won the Make Kentucky Colorful spring campaign.

"Are you telling people?" I asked them on our way over to the Wallflower Diner where Carla would announce if we won. My mom and dad were also hosting Carla's retirement party.

"We weren't, but I'm not sure if Grady can keep it a secret." Julia had a faint glow of pregnancy to her. Or maybe it was the look of satisfaction that she knew what was going on with her body.

We passed Social Knitwork.

"Are you taking classes from Leotta?" I questioned.

"I am. It was strange." Julia curled her arm in mine while the men walked behind us. "I was having some sort of desire to make a blanket, and I don't have a crafty bone in my body. Grady suggested a knitting class, and I jumped on it."

"Now we know why you had that feeling." I wanted to

touch her belly so bad, but I didn't. "Do you know how far along you are?"

"They said close to twelve weeks, and my body didn't even let me know it." She rolled her eyes. "But they say things are fine. The morning sickness should start to subside soon."

"I'm so happy." I snuggled up to her as we walked into the diner, which was filled with everyone we knew awaiting the big news.

"You're just in time." Iris had her eagle eyes on the door, waiting for us. "Carla just got the call." She pointed to the far corner where Carla was hunched over with the phone up to her ear.

"Your cake looks amazing." I couldn't stop looking at the dessert table that Pie in the Face, Iris's bakery and pie shop, had catered for the event.

The retirement cake Iris had made was a very cool suitcase cake with another small cake decorated like the globe and another cake on top of that. A big chocolate scripted mold atop the last cake read CONGRATU-LATIONS.

"Trust me, Carla knew exactly what she wanted." Iris's brows rose, then they lowered. "You have been having…." Her eyes slid to Mac. "Oh my goodness, Bernie!"

"Are you two okay?" Mac walked up and asked, not realizing what he walked into.

"You two," Iris gasped and wagged a finger between us.

"Stop it." I pushed her finger down.

"Yes. Iris. We two." Mac grinned hugely. "She's fantastic, and you're going to have to share her more with me."

Iris rubbed her hands together and started to give us some of her words of unwanted wisdom, but we were saved by Carla's much-awaited announcement.

"First, I'd like to thank everyone who did exactly everything I had asked. Unfortunately, Sugar Creek Gap didn't win the statewide award, but know that I couldn't've had a better send-off for my retirement." Carla's words fell over the crowd like a heavy blanket.

"Congratulations to Carla. We are so lucky to have had you as the beautification president all of these years." Iris always knew how to break a silence and bring a little cheer. "This is really a retirement party. So be sure you go grab your plate of food, and then we will be celebrating with cake!" Iris encouraged everyone to eat then turned to me and whispered, "Everything is better with cake."

"I'd like to skip the food and go straight for that cake," I said.

"No way. You've got a man now. You need to keep in shape." Iris and I started to laugh hard.

"It looks like someone is having a good time." Sheriff Angie said when she and Luke walked up. My suspicions about the two of them looked to be true. Maybe they didn't have a full relationship, but there was something brewing.

"We were just saying how we'd much rather go straight to the cake instead of the food." Iris was so quick witted, and I loved that about her.

"Luke." I gave him a soft smile to gauge where we stood.

"Bernadette." He clasped his hands behind his back and rocked back on his heels.

"I can see I was wrong about Carla," I told Angie when Luke had moved over to talk to Mac. "I did hear it was rat poison."

Angie's mouth opened, then she shut it, then opened it again, waiting a few seconds before she spoke.

"I guess you would know that now that you're Lee's

beneficiary." She looked at me. "Maybe I should ask you if you had access to rat poisoning."

"Really? Are you joking me?" I rolled my eyes. "Not me, but I know Walter Ward had a big ol' bottle of it spraying for rats over at Mac's house, which he's trying to sell, and it just so happens to be next to Lee's house."

I planted the seed. She looked as cool as a cucumber. But I could tell she was noodling over what I had said. I knew Angie so well that I could probably vomit what she was thinking word for word. And I had her thinking about Walter Ward having rat poison right next to the crime scene.

"I don't know if he did it or not, but I did hear him arguing with Lee when I was delivering the mail. Lee was very upset and told me he wanted everyone to leave him alone." I sighed as if I were just having a conversation with an old friend. No stress. "Say, do you know if your deputies picked up Lee's stamp collection? I can't find them anywhere."

"We didn't take any stamps, as far as I can recall." She folded her arms, cutting herself off from the world when Walter walked up.

"Just the woman I want to see," Walter told me in greeting. "I understand you're the owner of Lee Macum's house."

"I guess now that she owns my uncle's house, you don't have time for my phone calls." Luke hurried over when he saw Walter. "You are pathetic. You know, they call you an ambulance chaser, and now I see why."

The room fell silent. All eyes were on Luke and Walter.

"Listen, you're the one who called me about the house when you thought Lee was going to the nursing home." Walter wasn't about to take Luke's accusations lying down. "You're the one who needs a quick buck."

"It looks like to me you need the quick buck by going after the house with her." Luke jerked a finger at me. "And my uncle died of rat poison. I think I heard something about you spraying rat poison at the house next to my uncle's. Did you spray it down his throat?"

"Why don't we take this down to the station." A collective gasp waved across the room when Angie grabbed both men by the elbow and dragged them out the door.

Chapter 17

The little kerfuffle among Luke, Walter, and Angie during what was to be the celebratory party for Sugar Creek Gap's big number-one win for the Make Kentucky Colorful, which turned out to be a thank-you-so-much-for-your-service-type of retirement party for Carla, transformed that celebration into a gossip session about whether Luke or Walter killed Lee.

The news of my new grandchild also made for a good topic of conversation. Everyone found out when Julia had the worst bout of morning sickness and couldn't even make it into the bathroom. Mac had been amazing when I told him I was going to go home and get my things ready for the funeral and repass.

Mom had already made several different casseroles to bring, and I couldn't help but ask if she'd make her famous homemade rainforest crackers to go with the homemade chicken noodle soup in honor of Lee. Lee loved Mom's chicken noodle soup, and he always ordered extra rain-forest crackers to go with it.

Buster and Rowena were fast asleep after I made it

home. Buster ran out the door to do his business and wanted to sit and look at me when we got in bed. Rowena barely looked my way as if I were disturbing her beauty sleep. Thankful for both of my fur babies and also grateful for Grady, Julia, and my new grandbaby, I fell fast asleep, only to wake up later to the beeping alarm.

"Time to go potty," I told Buster, who'd already jumped out of the bed and waited for me to get up before he darted down the hall to the kitchen. I glanced over at Rowena, and her slit eyes told me she wasn't about to get up.

On my way down the hall, I flipped on the shower so my water would be nice and hot, grabbed my phone from the counter, and let Buster out the door. I quickly texted Monica to make sure she was still okay with taking my route today. Instead of her texting me back, she called.

"Good morning," I greeted her and was very grateful she was always willing to help out.

"Hey, Bernie. I'm sorry to call you, but I can't seem to find your key to your locker." I had given Monica one of the extra keys to my locker because I had kept really detailed notes in there about various pets I'd encountered along my route as well as who could have a treat, who couldn't, and who might bite.

I also had kept a log about the customers and little details about them so I could make their experiences a little more personal when I delivered their mail. I quickly grabbed my key ring and noticed I had an extra one on there.

"Let me grab a shower and I'll be there to give you another one," I told her.

"Oh no. I don't want you to have to come this early."

"It's fine. I was up and going to go to the diner to see if my mom needed any help getting any of the food over to

Luke's house for the repass. I'll be right down." I opened the door to let Buster back in.

It never really took me too long to get ready, but today I did apply makeup and fix my hair. Normally I'd never look in the mirror and call myself pretty, but today I felt pretty. Though it was a sad day, I felt so much joy inside. Not only because Lee had left me a wonderful letter but also because my life seemed to be becoming whole with Mac and now the baby entering my life.

I had decided to wear a black pant suit with a red scarf tied around my neck for a pop of color, figuring the pants would be a lot more comfortable than a dress and stockings. These days, I was more about comfort, and it was about Lee Macum.

Thinking about Lee made me wonder about Luke and Walter.

When I got into the car, I quickly texted Luke asking if there was anything I could do for him at the house before the repass.

"Good morning," I answered my phone without looking at the caller ID.

"Bernadette Butler?" The deep voice caught me off guard.

"Yes?" I questioned.

"This is Isiah Blackwell, the philatelist. I received your call. Is it too early to talk?" he questioned.

"No. As a matter of fact, I'm on my way into town for Lee's funeral at ten this morning." I wasn't sure why I felt the need to tell a man I didn't know exactly what I was doing. "Thank you for getting back to me."

"It's a shame that I never got to make the transaction with Lee. I'd been hounding him for years to get the stamp to complete my collection." Isiah had a very nice laugh on the other end of the line that made me smile. "He could be a picky man. One day he wanted to sell it to me, and the next day he did not."

"He definitely had a mind of his own. I'm actually his mail carrier, and we'd gotten to know each other over the course of the ten years." I started to go down memory lane like most people did when someone died.

"Then you know how much he loved that Pan-American stamp. I know there are several in the collection, but he has the one I need." Isiah had told me what to look for.

I knew the stamp but had never seen one in person, so I wasn't even sure I'd know it if I saw it.

"Did he tell you where he kept the stamp?" I asked.

"Tell me? I seen it." The deep laugh came out again. "It was the only thing he kept in that small safe of his."

"Safe?" I tried to refresh my memory about whether I'd seen a safe. I didn't remember one, but maybe Millie did.

"Yes. He bent down and had me go down to the ground with him. I'm not going to lie—I did fear those boxes were going to fall right down on us. I even asked him about why he lived liked that, and he simply said they were his life treasures." Isiah groaned. "I am glad I do not have the daunting task you do going through his house."

"When was the last time you talked to him about the stamp?" I asked, wondering if he'd been there a long time ago and Lee had gotten rid of the safe.

"A week ago. I came back to Sugar Creek Gap to get one more look at it to see if I wanted to pay his three-thousand-dollar asking price, even though it's only worth about twelve hundred."

Three thousand dollars? Would that amount be worth it for someone to have killed Lee?

"In fact, I had gotten the signed receipt stating my offer was picked up at the post office." That got my attention.

"Signed receipt? You had the offer sent certification?" I asked, knowing I could see who signed for it.

"Yes. Got confirmation yesterday, but the strange thing is that it didn't have Lee's signature. Someone by the name of Luke Macum signed for it."

Luckily, I'd turned into the post office parking lot because I nearly skidded the car to an abrupt halt.

"Luke?" I questioned to make sure I heard correctly even though I'd be sure to check on it myself.

"Mmhhmm. Got it right here. Want me to text you a photo?" he asked.

"Yes. Please." I put the car in park and sat there trying to process everything Isiah was telling me, which brought me right back to why I couldn't help but think Luke had everything to gain from killing Lee.

It all played out in my head as I recalled all the times I'd seen or even heard news about Luke. Luke asked Angie if his uncle was murdered. Why would he immediately ask her that when Lee could've died of natural causes?

Luke and Walter had that private conversation where Luke told Walter that he said he'd call, but Walter said he thought things might've changed... what did that mean?

Luke wanted Brother Don to go see Lee. Was that to conveniently make Luke look like some kind of caring nephew so when he did kill Lee no one, not even the sheriff, suspected him?

Luke also said Lee had been forgetting to lock his doors at night. Was he laying the foundation to throw everyone off that he really did kill Lee? If anyone had a key to Lee's house, it was probably Luke.

Then it smacked me in the face. Didn't one of the front porch ladies say something about them seeing Luke carrying something out of Lee's house? Wasn't that when they heard Lee and Luke fighting?

It was in my head to ask the front porch ladies about it when I saw them at Lee's viewing. If not there, I'd ask at the repass.

"Let me know if things change and you'd like to sell the stamp to me." Isiah was still talking about the stamp, from which I'd clearly moved on.

"Yeah. I'll be in touch." I hung up the phone.

I checked my texts before I went into the post office to see if Luke had texted me back, but he hadn't. Maybe he wasn't up, but it was almost nine o'clock, and he needed to be at the funeral home by nine-thirty.

Monica was standing up front with the other clerks waiting for me. I rolled the key off my key ring and gave it to her.

"Did you happen to give Luke Macum a certified letter for Lee?" I asked her, knowing she was the only clerk at the counter unless she was working someone's route, like today.

"You know about that?" Her mouth drew tight. "I had no idea Luke wasn't going to be the executor, and I know I'm supposed to hold all mail, but we are a small town, and we know everyone."

I gave her a hard stare.

"Yes," she answered. "I know. You don't want an explanation. You want an answer. Yes. He signed for it."

"That's all I needed to know." I turned to leave so I could get down to the funeral home.

"Am I in trouble?" she asked.

"Not from me. But I need to get that letter." I sucked in a deep breath. "And that safe."

Deep down, I knew the item Luke was seen carrying out of Lee's house had to be the safe. What else could it be? Not to mention, Isiah had said there was a small safe and he had to bend down to look in it with Lee. I didn't forget him mentioning the boxes and them falling on him. That empty space where Lee's coffee cup had rolled under had to be where the safe was.

The coffee cup.

"Nah." I tried to shake off the idea of Luke bringing Lee a cup of coffee with the rat poison in it. I gulped. "I'm sorry, Lee," I whispered when I knew I would have to use his viewing service and the repass as a way to sleuth my way around Luke's house. I had to do it not only to find the safe and the certified letter but also the rat poison.

I tried to put all the thoughts in the back of my head when I walked into the funeral home. After Jigs met me at the door with the bill, that fueled my fire even more about Luke. I was itching to get out of here so I could get to his house and look around while he wasn't there.

The viewing ceremony was much more of a memorial service. It was actually very nice. Lee had asked to be cremated in his will, and since his body was just released, Jigs hadn't been able to fulfill Lee's wishes in such a short period of time. Since Jigs had assumed Lee was going to be laid out when we'd spoken, he had simply laid out the clothes Luke had chosen and set them on a chair with a nice photo of Lee that Luke had framed.

The flowers were overflowing, and the crowd was large. It was apparent how many lives Lee had touched as their garbage man of many years. Brother Don said a really nice speech about the afterlife and our eternal home before he opened the room up for the mourners to say something if they wanted to.

I stood in the back and kept my eye on Luke the entire time. He sat there as if he really did care about Lee when all I could think about was how he knew he shouldn't have signed for that certified letter and how he knew the last time he'd seen Lee, they'd been arguing.

"You were wrong again." Angie Hafley walked up beside me.

"I barely noticed it was you in that dress." I smiled. "You look nice. What was I wrong about?" I took her bait.

"Walter Ward." She looked at me out of the side of her eye. "Lee's time of poisoning was placed at around eight p.m. Walter was clear in Lexington when Lee was poisoned. Not only that, but he was with one of Amy Logsdon's employees from that morning working on his client's yards to get them all pretty for the Make Kentucky Colorful campaign, and that same employee went with him to Lexington to see about a job because Amy is thinking about expanding the business outside of Sugar Creek Gap."

The news of Logsdon Landscaping trying to grow didn't come as a surprise. Amy had taken over her family company to try to save it from going out of business. But the part about Walter only made me think Luke did it.

Angie didn't bother waiting to see my response. She walked up the center aisle and took the seat next to Luke.

I wanted to tell Angie so badly what I had found out and my theories on Luke, but she looked so chummy with him that I knew she wouldn't hear of it. Not today anyways.

One by one, customers on Lee's garbage route got up and talked nicely about him. How he did things that weren't in his job description, like the time he would take the elderly citizens' cans back to their houses or even the time one of them was looking to replace an old TV stand but couldn't afford to buy one. Lee had found one on his route in someone's garbage and took it back to them.

If I wanted to get to the repass before Luke and snoop around, I knew I'd better say a few words then dart out of there using the excuse that my mom needed me to help set up the food.

"I only wanted to say a few words. We all have heard from Lee's customers and friends how kind he was. I don't need to tell you that, but the one thing I will say is how the town knew Lee had kept more than he threw out." There was a collective murmur of laughter and nodding along with some smiles. I adjusted the microphone to fit my height. "Lee had written me a letter." I pulled Lee's letter out of my pantsuit, placed the letter on the podium, and smoothed it out with my hands. Out of the corner of my eye, Luke shifted in his seat. "I'm not going to read the full letter, but I do want you to hear this one line. I know we've all heard it so many times before, but after listening to all the good deeds he did when he listened to what the needs of his customers were, I found this to be fitting. *Ahem.*" I cleared my throat. "One man's trash is another man's treasures."

I looked around the room and knew it applied to the customer that needed that TV stand and the other customer who said her son needed any furniture. Lee had brought them an entire bedroom suite, though none of it matched. Still, Lee understood the impact that one statement made, and I left everyone with that one quote.

Chapter 18

"There you are." My mom greeted me with an exhausted look on her face as she stood in the middle of Luke's small kitchen. "Did you see the crowd at the viewing? I hope I have enough food."

"I'm sure it'll be fine." I bounced on my toes. "Which way is the bathroom?" I asked her, pretending I had to go potty.

"How do I know?" She moved around the kitchen, opening some of the cabinets. She curled up on her toes to see if what she was looking for was lurking in the back. "I've never been here."

"Okay." I looked down the hall at all the closed doors. "I'll go find it."

Mom was too busy looking to even hear me, so I took off down the hall in search for the safe, letter, and rat poison.

"Bernie!" I heard someone call my name when I tried to quickly walk past the family room full of people already there.

I closed my eyes, sucked in a deep breath, and twirled

to face the crowd. When I opened my eyes, the front porch ladies were in a huddle near the front door, all dressed to the nines in their Sunday-go-to-church-meeting clothes. Each one of them wore a different colored pastel mid-calf skirt with a matching jacket. A small purse dangled from each woman's gripped hands, and the ladies' matching pill box hats were like cake toppers that sealed their outfits.

"Bernie!" Millie yelled again, waving me over.

"Hi, ladies." I greeted each one with a small hug. "I'm so glad you could make it. Listen…" I glanced around to make sure no one was listening. "Tell me again who you saw coming and going from Lee's house. Unfortunately, Carla and Walter have been taken off the suspect list."

"What about Luke?" Mille asked.

"That's what I'm trying to find out. Apparently, he signed for a certified letter for Lee about a stamp, and that's illegal, since he's not the executor of the estate." I knew they all knew this since they were all widowed. But saying these words out loud added fuel to my fire. "And I have reason to believe there was a small safe in the area where I found Lee's coffee cup. Which reminds me, did anyone bring him coffee that day?"

"Gosh. Well, there was Carla who came by, Walter, and Luke. But you're saying they are all off the suspect list." Millie blinked several times.

"Not Luke," I reminded her.

"And I don't remember anyone bringing Lee coffee." She looked as if she were trying to remember. "But he always had a coffee. It was kinda gross too." Millie snarled. "He liked to keep the same cup all day and then heat it up through the day. And if he made a pot of coffee and the automatic power turned off, he would run that old coffee back through the pot."

The thought of that made my stomach curl. I was

thankful I'd never taken him up on the offer for a cup of coffee on my route.

"If Luke did take the safe, does that make him the killer?" Harriette made a good point I wish she didn't make.

"Then we need to find that rat poison," I told them and turned around, only to hear them shuffle behind me.

The five of us each took a different door to look in once we were down the hall and away from prying eyes. I knew we were on limited time and had only a matter of minutes before Luke got home after thanking everyone at the viewing for attending. He might have even been giving his address so they could all stop by for some food.

I opened the door to the office. I hurried over to the desk and immediately noticed the last stamp I'd given Lee from my father the day before I found him. I frantically looked on the top of the desk to see if I could find anything else like the certified letter. Just because he had the stamp didn't mean he was a killer, but he could be brought up on charges for signing that letter. If only I could find out.

I heard some sort of bird chirping. I looked out the window to see if I could find what the heck kind of bird was outside.

"Bernadette? Why are you in my office?" Luke was standing in the door of his office.

"Cuckoooooo." Gertrude was behind him waving her hand. "Cuckooooo...." She clamped her mouth. I glared. "I didn't know how to signal you were in danger."

"Bernie." Angie walked up behind Luke. "What is going on?"

By the time she finished her question, all the front porch ladies were in the room.

"He killed Lee," Millie accused and pointed her finger at Luke.

"Killed my uncle?" He laughed. "I sure hope Violet has that room open at the nursing home because Millie has lost her mind."

"You better watch your mouth," I told him sternly. "Angie, I know there's something going on between you two, but you have to hear me out."

"Bernie." Angie's lack of approval was written all over her face.

"This stamp was given to Lee by my dad. I personally delivered it. And there's a certified letter Luke signed for, but it's Lee's, and it's illegal." I drew my eyes to look at Luke. He shifted his weight from left to right as he crossed his arms. "He also had been trying to get Lee deemed unable to care for himself so that he had to move out of his house."

"Why on earth would Luke want that dump?" She practically laughed me off.

"Because he is hurting for money. He can't pay his cat checkup bill, and he can't pay his taxes. He needed the money from the sale of the stamps, one stamp in particular." I took Isiah's business card out of my pocket and handed it to her. "This man can tell you all about the stamps in the safe Luke took from Lee when he was living. When Lee didn't want him to."

So I might've added the last part about Lee not giving it to Luke. He might've. I was not sure, but from how I read the letter Lee left me, he had no intention of giving Luke the stamp.

"Is she right? Did you take a safe?" Angie looked at Luke.

"Yeah. He didn't need the money. I took the safe." Luke walked over to a closet and opened it. There sat the small safe that would fit perfectly in the empty space I'd seen at Lee's. "But I didn't kill my uncle. Yes, I signed for the letter, but it was before I knew I wasn't going to be named executor. I took care of my uncle. I didn't want him to die. I wanted him to be taken care of and not in that filthy house." He put his wrists out. "Go ahead, take me to the station and give me a lie detector. I don't even have rat poison."

Everyone turned around when we heard another person walk into the room. It was Matilda Garrison with a tray full of coffees.

"Oops." She looked shocked. "It looks like I've walked in on something. I brought Lee's favorite coffee for my little contribution for the repass." She started to walk backwards out of the room.

"I'll take one." Angie lifted her hand in the air. "I hope he liked it strong."

"Yes, he did," Matilda confirmed and gave everyone a cup of coffee from her tray. "I'll let y'all get back to whatever it was you were discussing."

When Matilda slipped out of the room, Angie asked the front porch ladies to leave her, Luke, and me alone.

"Luke, please open the safe." Angie was calm, cool and collected.

Luke took the safe out of the closet and set it on his desk. He took his billfold out of his pants pocket to retrieve the safe code from it.

"So you did take the safe?" I questioned him.

"No. Yes. Well, only because Uncle Lee wanted me to get the safe open so he could get the Pan-American stamp to show the stamp collector. He had heard from Carla a few weeks ago that I'd gone to see Vivian at the nursing home, and he was upset. I'd gone to the nursing home to check out prices and if he could afford it. So Uncle Lee knew I'd gone there a couple of times, which I guess is when he'd gone to change his will." Luke bent down and turned the small dial on the safe, keeping his eyes on the numbers on the piece of paper.

"So you went to talk to Vivian a few times before I saw you there this week?" I asked, since he was probably right about Lee changing his will a few weeks ago.

"Yes. Carla had told him during one of her visits with the city's finest that she loved to deliver. In fact, she told him that she wasn't going to bother him anymore about cleaning up his property because in a few weeks he was going to live in a nursing home." The sound of the safe lock clicked.

The three of us held our breath when he opened it. There was a single stamp in a plastic stamp case. That was the only thing in the small safe.

"That's what is so expensive?" Angie took it from him.

"Yeah. I mean, a few thousand dollars, which would help me pay my current bills." He looked at the stamp in her hand. "He was going to sell the stamp. That's what we fought over. But I didn't kill him. I might need money, but I needed my family more."

"Bernadette, I'm sure you have figured out Luke and I have been dating." She turned to Luke. "It might come as a shock, and I know we were together at Lee's time of death and the hours Jigs had put the time of ingestion of poison, but I still did take a look around your house when we were here yesterday."

Okay. Well, that came as a shock. I did know they had something between them, but her actually thinking that he might've killed his uncle was a bold move that I didn't think Angie even considered.

"I didn't find any sort of rat poison. I also looked through all of your receipts to see if you'd bought any rat poison, and I might've gone down to the hardware store to see if they'd remembered you coming in." Her words made Luke's face contort into all different expressions. "But that's part of dating a sheriff." She laid the stamp on the table.

"Yeah. Well"—Luke ran his hand through his hair —"if that's part of dating you, I guess I can live with it."

From what Angie had said, Luke didn't kill Lee, but who did?

"I'm going to have to take the stamp and give it to Bernadette because legally, it's hers." She used a finger to push it toward me. "And we have this little matter about the certified letter."

"I didn't know Bernadette was going to be the one he named as beneficiary, so I didn't think I was doing anything wrong." Luke had a point.

"Really." I looked at Angie. "Honestly, there was no harm done. He didn't call the stamp collector because I did talk to him and was more than happy to pass along his information to you. And he didn't sell the stamp, so I wouldn't want to press any charges."

There was a look of relief on his face.

"I really want to find out who killed him," I told her, knowing that all three of my suspects had been cleared.

"I hate to say it, but is it possible he accidentally poisoned himself?" Luke asked, his brows furrowed. "As much as people don't want to believe it, he was having memory issues. He started to live like a homeless person. I caught him eating Buster's dog food. He recycled his day-old coffee unless someone brought him a cup."

"Fine. I will look into all that. But right now, you two have a repass to host." Angie looked to be at her wits' end. "We do have a few leads that might bring us some more information, but in the meantime, I'm asking the two of you to let me do my job."

"Fine." I only agreed because I was at a dead end.

"Do you know what you're going to do with the house?" Luke asked on our way back down the hall.

"No." I shook my head. "But if there is anything you truly want in the house, you can have it."

"There are some family photo albums in one of those boxes. I'd love to have those." Luke did have a tender side that was hitting my soft spot.

"Of course. Just be sure you clear it with Angie first." I wanted to make sure Angie was definitely done with the house even though she'd cleared.

The living room and kitchen were filled with citizens who had come to pay their last respects to Lee. Times like these were when I loved living in Sugar Creek Gap. The community came together, no matter how they felt about Lee and his hoarding issues. Even some of his customers on his garbage route were there.

I moseyed around and stopped to listen to a few of the stories they were telling and thanked them for coming. Lee had touched more lives than either Luke or I had realized.

"Would you like another cup of Lee's blend?" Matilda asked when I walked up to talk to her and Carla, who were standing alone in the hallway between the kitchen and living room.

"Lee's blend?" I asked.

"Yes." Carla smiled. "Lee and I might've had our differences, but we did like the same blend Matilda served, so I just so happened to tell her she should rename it."

"I think that's a great idea." I couldn't believe Carla had it in her to be nice about Lee.

"We were just talking about how Carla was probably the last person who bought Lee a cup of coffee before he died." Matilda gave a soft smile to Carla. "If I hadn't known he was poisoned, I'd think Carla might've killed him with kindness." She joked, but I didn't find it so funny.

"You did?" I questioned. "You took him a coffee the morning before I found him?"

"Yes. I did." She gave me a stern look. "It was my last-ditch offer for a peace offering to get him to clean up that house. But you can see what good all that did me. We lost."

"Mm-hhmmm." I gulped and remembered Millie telling me how Lee would let the coffee sit and then reheat it throughout the day. "If you'll excuse me."

I couldn't help but get the idea that Carla could've still killed Lee. I started to sweat and frantically look around the room for Millie or any of the front porch ladies. When I didn't see them in the family room or kitchen, I slipped past Matilda and Carla to head back down the hall and see if they had gone into Luke's office.

The office was empty.

"Are you okay?" Carla was standing in the doorway of the office when I turned around to leave.

"I'm fine." I pinched a smile and recognized her sincere-sounding question wasn't quite as sincere as she wanted it to be. "I guess I'm confused about why you would bring a coffee to Lee after you'd been hounding him for months about his house and then telling him about Luke going to talk to Vivian at the nursing home. It just seems odd."

"Odd that I finally resorted to trying to be kind to the old fool? Honestly, Bernadette, your mother has always taught you a little kindness goes a long way." Carla's face contorted; her brows lifted. "Seriously, did you see that mess?"

Chills spread up my body. I gulped.

"You poisoned Lee. You got him a coffee and somehow

poisoned it with rat poison." As I said that, images of the rat poison sitting on the front porch of Mac's house, the one Walter was selling, came into my mind. "You walked up onto the porch next door and you poisoned it."

"Oh, Bernadette. Honey," she scoffed. "I know people around town have talked about how you've changed and kinda lost your marbles since Richard died and then you had to hear he'd cheated on you your entire marriage, but to resort to calling me a killer now?"

"This." I pointed a finger at her. "This is your ammunition. You use your nasty hateful words to get what you want, and when you don't get your way…" I hesitated. "Oh my gosh, you and Lee had another fight. You didn't give a coffee the first time you went." I recalled Millie telling me that she'd seen Carla show up at Lee's house twice that day. "You went back with a coffee, and that was when you poisoned it. You walked right up to the porch next to Lee's, put rat poison in the coffee, and decided to hand it to him."

"Listen to me," Carla said through her gritted teeth. Her eyes snapped as she got closer to me. Her hand tugged on a piece of her hair. "I gave him multiple chances. He refused to help out our town."

"The coffee cup." I gasped and brought my hand up to my mouth when I remembered the coffee cup in the negative space where the safe had sat. "When you went into the house with me, you tried to throw away the coffee cup from the Roasted Bean. I told you to leave it all there."

Her chest heaved up and down, her glare got harder, and her jaw clenched. She moved closer to the desk. She shifted her gaze down, and I could see it fix on the scissors.

"That's the coffee cup that you gave him. The sheriff couldn't put you at the scene, because he didn't drink it right away. Lee is known to heat and reheat his coffee, which is why the poison didn't kill him until hours later after he'd finished that cup of coffee." My eyes darted back and forth from her clenched fists to the scissors as I noticed her eyes shift.

I could tell by the look on her face and the meanness in her eyes that I'd figured it out and she was trying to figure out what to do in this situation.

"You know, I never really liked you." She grabbed the pair of scissors from the desk and ran toward me at full force.

"Help!" I screamed and grabbed Carla's forearm before she lunged forward and tried to stab me with the scissors. I pushed her to the right and tried to get around her to the left.

She continued to swing her arm around and at me, with the scissors jabbing at any part of me she could try to stab.

"You won't get away with killing me! Help!" I screamed. "Help me!"

Her eyes were wide open. Her nostrils were flared as she breathed in and out at a rapid pace. Her back was hunched over as she tried to figure out my next move.

The madness in her eyes told me her normal person wasn't present in the situation and she would try her best to kill me.

"Carla," I tried to say in a calm voice when I thought no one could hear me over all the people in the house and the chatter going on. "Let's think about this." I held my hands out and moved right when she moved left and vice versa.

"I've thought long and hard about him and this for months. I did this for the good of our community." Carla seemed to believe she had done Sugar Creek Gap a great deed.

Over her shoulder, I could see from the corner of my eye that Angie had opened the door. She put her finger up to her mouth for me to stay quiet.

"Lee Macum was an eye sore, and I got rid of the problem. Now you have a new house. You can live by your boyfriend." Carla stood up straight. "We can keep this little secret ours, Bernadette. Look at it as if I did you a favor." An evil smile curled up on her face. "Isn't Julia pregnant with your first grandbaby? Wouldn't you want them to live in a nice home? Have a good neighborhood? See, that's what I did for you. I killed Lee. He left you the house, and now your grandbaby will have a home and not some apartment above a diner. You have me to thank for that."

"Don't you dare bring up my family in your murder. We don't need your help." I pointed at Angie. Carla jumped around.

"Angie." Carla put the scissors down. "Bernadette killed Lee. She knew he was leaving his house to her, and she found out Grady is having a baby and wanted the house for them. Lee told her no, and she used the poison on the front porch of Mac's house next to Lee to poison him with the food she's always bringing him. She killed Lee Macum."

Was she really turning this on me? I blinked in bafflement.

"I had to grab the scissors because she was threatening to kill me if I told you that I figured out who killed him." Carla pointed at me. "Arrest her!"

Angie reached around and took the badge out of her back pocket.

"You'll find the murder weapon in a garbage bag in Lee's house. A coffee cup," I said.

"What?" Carla glared at me. "I didn't kill him. She did."

"Carla Ramey, you are under arrest for poisoning and killing Lee Macum." Angie started to read all the rights over Carla's protest as she guided her out of the house and into her sheriff's car.

Everyone had walked out of the house, spilling into Luke's front yard, a little confused about what was going on. Murmurs softly crossed everyone's lips, and a few shrugs rose from the crowd as we all stood there watching Angie pull off with Carla in the back seat.

"Looks like she's going from the beautification committee to jail." Millie couldn't stop smiling.

Chapter 19

From what I'd heard, it took Carla Ramey a few hours to finally confess to killing Lee Macum. Angie had gone back to Lee's house and picked up the garbage bag. Jigs Baker had used some sort of technology to get a test run on the dried-up coffee in the bottom of the cup. That way, Angie could have a way to see any poison was in there before she sent the coffee off the crime lab.

I'd even received a call from Iris. She has volunteered me to help her with the bridal shower Zeke Grey was hosting. The front porch ladies were going to die when they found out. I actually missed my regular route and my normal routine. I couldn't wait until the morning when I got back to my customers.

"How did you figure all of that out?" Grady asked me from the table as he helped Julia snap the green beans so we could get them on the stove and cook them for the Sunday family supper. Rowena was sitting on the bench next to Julia. Buster was waiting for a green bean to accidentally fall on the floor. I had to admit, since he moved in with me, my floor was very clean. Rowena wouldn't be caught dead eating something off the floor.

"Carla had come over to help me clean up the yard the morning the judges were coming because she knew it'd been willed to me." I went to the back door to let Mac in.

"Hey." He greeted me with a smile and gave me a nice soft kiss on the lips when he came inside.

"Hey." I couldn't help smiling. Being around Mac gave me all the warm, fuzzy feelings that I'd longed to have.

"I saw your parents coming up the driveway." He handed me a dish. Buster trotted next to him. "I'll go help them in. Iris dropped off a pie to bring. She said she can't make it to supper."

Mac and Buster headed back out the door to go help my parents bring whatever they were going to bring for supper. Mom never told me, but most of the time she brought something left over from the diner or combined ingredients to make something. Either way, Sunday supper with the family was my favorite time of the week. I loved being around my family, and now that my relationship with Mac had drastically changed, it was even more special.

Mom had brought fried pork chops. We ended having way too much food.

"How about a slice of Iris's pie with a nice cup of coffee?" I stood up from the table after everyone had eaten and started brewing coffee in the coffee maker. "While the coffee brews, I have something to say."

I grabbed the manila envelope from the counter and took it over to the table so everyone could see me.

My eyes teared up when I looked at Mom, Dad, Mac, Grady, and Julia gathered around my table. Of course Rowena was still sleeping on the bench next to Julia, and Buster was keeping an eye on the floor hoping something would drop.

"As you all know, Lee Macum has left all of his belongings to me." I opened the top of the envelope and slipped out the papers. "I have given all the contents of the house to Luke. He is much in need of the items to sell, and that includes Lee's stamp collection. I have decided that Rowena, Buster, and I are going to move into Lee's house."

Grady's jaw dropped.

"Mom, this is our family home." He reached over and put his hand on Julia's belly. "I want my child to experience everything you let me experience."

"Hear me out," I told him. "I am giving you and Julia the farm."

Julia gasped. Grady's jaw dropped again.

"I want the two of you to experience the farm with your family. This way, you can grow as you want to and do all the things you love." I watched as my son and his wife hugged.

My parents held hands on top of the table.

"Mac has already agreed to help me pick out new fixtures for Lee's house that'll suit me and with any sort of architectural needs I might have. It's perfect for me to get to work. It's a small two-bedroom home that's going to be perfect for me. Also, I'll be close to Mom and Dad." I looked at my parents.

My dad patted Mac on the back.

"You did good, kid," my dad said.

"I only have you and Mom to thank." I looked between my parents, then back at my son.

I said a little silent prayer for Lee Macum. I hated that Lee had died, and I'd like to think that even if he hadn't died and left his house to me, I would've still given Grady and Julia the farmhouse and moved into the apartment over the diner.

"What are you thinking?" Mac got out of his chair and came over to stand next to me.

Mom and Dad were busy talking to Julia and Grady about any changes to the house they'd like to make.

"I'm thinking life is pretty great." I looked up at him. "If you would've told me a few months ago that I was going to inherit a house on your street and would also become a grandmother soon, I wouldn't have believed you."

"Would you believe it if I told you that I've been in love with you for many years?" He looked down at me and smiled.

"Mac Tabor." I put my arm around him. "I think you were right after all these years."

"What about?" he asked and tugged me closer.

"You always said I picked the wrong best friend to marry," I teased, remembering how he'd say in front of Richard, "Bernie, you picked the wrong guy."

"I don't think it would come as a surprise to Richard that I'm pursuing you now." He bent down and kissed me.

I wanted to tell him that I knew Richard wouldn't be surprised. But I kept the little secret that Richard would always tell me—that if anything ever happened to him, he wanted me to end up with Mac Tabor.

It looked like everyone in my life was finally getting everything they'd ever wanted. And really… all we ever wanted was to be surrounded by love.

Want to continue your vacation in Sugar Creek Gap?
The next book in the series, ALL SHE WROTE is
available for preorder and will be released May 26th.
CLICK HERE! And read on for a sneak peek.

RECIPES

Bonbon Cookies
-submitted by Linda Swann

Chocolate Crinkles

Chocolate Chip Blonde

BonBon Cookies
submitted by Linda Swann

INGREDIENTS

1/2cup soft butter

3/4cup sifted confectioners' sugar

1 Tbsp. Vanilla

1 1/8 cup sifted flour

1/8 tsp salt

Fillings can be candied or well drained maraschino cherries

pitted dates or

gumdrops

DIRECTIONS

1. Thoroughly cream butter and sugar; stir in vanilla.
2. Mix in by hand ,the flour and salt.
3. Wrap a level tablespoon of dough around your filling.
4. Place 1 inch apart on a ungreased baking sheet.
5. Bake 350 degrees for 12-15 minutes until cookies are set, but not brown.

Chocolate Crinkles

INGREDIENTS

9 oz (270 g) dark chocolate, chopped, divided
2 large eggs, at room temperature
½ cup (100 g) granulated sugar
1 tsp (5 mL) vanilla extract
1 tsp (5 mL) balsamic vinegar
1 cup (130 g) icing sugar, plus extra for rolling cookies
½ cup (60 g) cocoa powder
1 Tbsp (7 g) cornstarch
½ tsp (2.5 g) salt

DIRECTIONS

1. Preheat the oven to 375 °F (190 °C). Line 2 baking trays with parchment paper.

2. Melt 6 oz (180 g) of the chocolate in a metal bowl placed over a saucepan filled with an inch of barely simmering water, stirring gently until melted. Set aside.

3. With electric beaters or in a stand mixer fitted with the whip attachment, whip the eggs with the granulated sugar, vanilla and Balsamic until frothy and light, about 3 minutes (it doesn't have to hold a "ribbon"). Whisk in the melted chocolate.

4. Sift in the icing sugar, cocoa powder, cornstarch and salt and stir in by hand until well combined. Stir in the remaining 3 oz of chopped chocolate. The batter may

seem very soft at first, but just give it a minute – it will tighten up.

5. Place some icing sugar in a shallow dish. Use a small ice cream scoop to scoop the batter and drop it directly into the icing sugar, rolling to coat each scoop fully.

6. Arrange these on the prepared baking trays, leaving 1 ½-inches between them.

7. Gently press each cookie flat with the palm of your hand. Bake the cookies for 10 minutes and cool the cookies on the tray just until they can be lifted off then cool on a rack.

Chocolate Chip Blondes

Ingredients

   2/3 cup creamy peanut butter
   1/2 cup packed brown sugar
   1/4 cup sugar
   1/4 cup unsweetened applesauce
   2 large eggs
   1 teaspoon vanilla extract
   1 cup gluten-free all-purpose baking flour
   1-1/4 teaspoons baking powder
   1 teaspoon xanthan gum
   1/4 teaspoon salt
   1/2 cup semisweet chocolate chips
   1/4 cup salted peanuts, chopped

Directions

1.In a large bowl, combine the peanut butter, sugars and applesauce.

   2.Beat in eggs and vanilla until blended. Combine the flour, baking powder, xanthan gum and salt; gradually add to peanut butter mixture and mix well.

   3. Stir in chocolate chips and peanuts.

   4. Put in a 9-in. square baking pan coated with cooking spray.

   5. Bake at 350° for 20-25 minutes or until a toothpick inserted in the center comes out clean.

   6. Cool on a wire rack and cut into squares.

PEPPER COOKIES

INGREDIENTS AND SIMPLE DIRECTIONS

Beat together:
- 1 cup shortening
- 3 eggs
- 1 1/4 cup sugar
- 1/2 cup milk

ADD:
- 4 cups flour
- 1/2 cup cocoa
- 4 tsp baking powder
- 1/2 tsp pepper
- 1/2 tsp cinnamon
- 1/2 tsp nutmeg
- 1/2 tsp cloves
- 1/2 tsp salt

ADD :

1 bag of chocolate chips and 1 1/2 cup chopped nuts. Roll into little balls and bake on a cookie sheet at 350 for 12-14 minutes. Let cool for about ten minutes before you enjoy them!

Like this book?
Tap here to leave a review now!
Join Tonya's newsletter to stay updated with new releases,
get free novels, access to exclusive bonus content, and
more!

Join Tonya's newsletter here.
Tap here to see all of Tonya's books.
Join all the fun on her Reader Group on Facebook.

Also By Tonya Kappes

Magical Cures Mystery Series
A CHARMING CRIME
A CHARMING CURE
A CHARMING POTION (novella)
A CHARMING WISH
A CHARMING SPELL
A CHARMING MAGIC
A CHARMING SECRET
A CHARMING CHRISTMAS (novella)
A CHARMING FATALITY
A CHARMING DEATH (novella)
A CHARMING GHOST
A CHARMING HEX
A CHARMING VOODOO
A CHARMING CORPSE
A CHARMING MISFORTUNE
A CHARMING BLEND (CROSSOVER WITH A KILLER COFFEE COZY)

A Camper and Criminals Cozy Mystery
BEACHES, BUNGALOWS, & BURGLARIES
DESERTS, DRIVERS, & DERELICTS
FORESTS, FISHING, & FORGERY
CHRISTMAS, CRIMINALS, & CAMPERS
MOTORHOMES, MAPS, & MURDER
CANYONS, CARAVANS, & CADAVERS
ASSAILANTS, ASPHALT, & ALIBIS
VALLEYS, VEHICLES & VICTIMS
SUNSETS, SABBATICAL, & SCANDAL
TENTS, TRAILS, & TURMOIL
KICKBACKS, KAYAKS, & KIDNAPPING

Killer Coffee Mystery Series
SCENE OF THE GRIND
MOCAH AND MURDER
FRESHLY GROUND MURDER
COLD BLOODED BREW
DECAFFEINATED SCANDAL
A KILLER LATTE
HOLIDAY ROAST MORTEM
DEAD TO THE LAST DROP
A CHARMING BLEND NOVELLA (CROSSOVER
WITH MAGICAL CURES MYSTERY)

Mail Carrier Cozy Mystery
STAMPED OUT
ADDRESS FOR MURDER
ALL SHE WROTE
RETURN TO SENDER
FIRST CLASS KILLER

A Ghostly Southern Mystery Series
A GHOSTLY UNDERTAKING
A GHOSTLY GRAVE
A GHOSTLY DEMISE
A GHOSTLY MURDER
A GHOSTLY REUNION
A GHOSTLY MORTALITY
A GHOSTLY SECRET
A GHOSTLY SUSPECT

A Southern Cake Baker Series
(WRITTEN UNDER MAYEE BELL)
CAKE AND PUNISHMENT
BATTER OFF DEAD

Also By Tonya Kappes

Kenni Lowry Mystery Series
FIXIN' TO DIE
SOUTHERN FRIED
AX TO GRIND
SIX FEET UNDER
DEAD AS A DOORNAIL
TANGLED UP IN TINSEL
DIGGIN' UP DIRT

Spies and Spells Mystery Series
SPIES AND SPELLS
BETTING OFF DEAD
GET WITCH or DIE TRYING

A Laurel London Mystery Series
CHECKERED CRIME
CHECKERED PAST
CHECKERED THIEF

A Divorced Diva Beading Mystery Series
A BEAD OF DOUBT SHORT STORY
STRUNG OUT TO DIE
CRIMPED TO DEATH

Olivia Davis Paranormal Mystery Series
SPLITSVILLE.COM
COLOR ME LOVE (novella)
COLOR ME A CRIME

About Tonya

Tonya has written over 65 novels, all of which have graced numerous bestseller lists, including the USA Today. Best known for stories charged with emotion and humor and filled with flawed characters, her novels have garnered reader praise and glowing critical reviews. She lives with her husband and a very spoiled rescue cat named Ro. Tonya grew up in the small southern Kentucky town of Nicholasville. Now that her four boys are grown men, Tonya writes full-time.

Learn more about her books here. Find her on Facebook, Twitter, BookBub, and her website.

Sign up to receive her newsletter, where you'll get free books, exclusive bonus content, and news of her releases and sales.

If you liked this book, please take a few minutes to leave a review now! Authors (Tonya included) really appreciate this, and it helps draw more readers to books they might like. Thanks!

Copyright

Made in United States
North Haven, CT
21 June 2023

38044970R00117